Hating You

A BLACKTHORN ELITE NOVEL

USA Today Bestselling Author
J.L. BECK
C. HALLMAN

1

WILLOW

"*I didn't do it. I didn't fucking do it.*" Brett's voice echoes in my mind. The image of him being taken out of the court room plays behind my closed eyes. I wake up drenched from head to toe in sweat, my heart racing inside my chest, beating against my rib cage like it might break free and fly away. I don't remember the last time I had a nightmare like this. Sitting up in my bed, I shove the covers off my clammy body and force air into my lungs, reminding myself that I did the right thing.

You're a good person, Willow. You know it was him. You did the right thing. I tell myself as I drag my butt into the shower and get ready for the day. Thank God these dorms have bathrooms attached to each room. I guess that's to be expected in one of the most elite universities in the country.

Washing my hair and body on autopilot, I rinse off and step out, grabbing a fluffy towel off the rack.

There is a small brunch event for all the freshmen and their families, and if I'm late... Shivers ripple down my back at the thought. After all the things my father did to get me into this school, I don't want to think of what might happen to me if I mess this up.

"You'll do right by our family name. You won't make a mockery out of me like your sister did, will you?" My father's stern voice rings out through my ears as a reminder of what's to come. Even after everything my sister had gone through, he still blamed her, still disowned her. Now she has nothing, and I'm forced to live up to my father's incredibly high standards. Then again, it's this or allow my sister to be homeless.

The only plus side to being here is that it's a two-hour drive from my father's estate to Blackthorn, and I doubt he will attend any of the family events, nor does he expect me to come home for the weekends. Thank God for that.

Alice, my roommate, groans into her pillow, her silky blonde hair nothing more than a knotted mess on her head. "It's morning already? It feels like I hardly slept," she groans.

"You literally drank like three Starbucks Espressos last night. I'm shocked you went to bed at all," I snort.

"It's not my fault your definition of water and mine are two different things," she yawns as she slowly pushes from the bed. "I need coffee to function, okay? Don't hate."

My lips turn up into a tiny smile, and I laugh softly. Alice is everything I'm not; lighthearted, funny, comes from a loving family. She doesn't have a care in the world, while I carry so many burdens, my back hurts.

She is, the glass is half-full, kind of person, while I'm, the glass is always half-empty, kind. Maybe we are a case of opposites attract because, since the moment I walked into the dorms, we hit it off. Alice introduced herself with a bright smile on her face, and like two magnets, we were drawn to each other. She's only been my roommate for a week, but we've already grown closer than I thought possible.

When I arrived at Blackthorn, I had very low expectations when it came to making friends. Back home, I had a plethora of friends; girls and guys. I was the popular girl, just like my sister had been. But all of that changed one night two years ago.

After everyone found out about what happened to my sister, everything fell apart. People stopped talking to me and turned their backs on us. They passed me in the school hallway like I was nothing more than a stranger, whispering to their friends. I'd be lying if I said I wasn't hurt by it, but honestly, I got over it. I don't need people to pretend to be my friends. If they are not real friends, then they are not worthy of being my friend at all.

"Is your dad coming to the freshman welcome brunch?" Tensing at the mention of my father, I shake my head.

"No, he's got to work, and it's too long of a drive for him to make out here."

"Oh, sorry. I thought I might get to meet your family," she chimes, blissfully unaware of what an ass my dad is. I haven't told her any of my family drama yet, and I don't think I will, not anytime soon at least. I would like to keep at least one person as a friend.

Getting dressed quickly, I tug on a pair of black skinny jeans and a pink blouse, then I look at myself in the mirror. With my long black hair still wet and clinging to my shoulders, I look like a drowned cat.

Alice goes into the bathroom to shower. I start drying the mangled strands of hair, using the brush to straighten them out as I go and then apply some light makeup, using the mirror in our room.

Twenty minutes later, like the beauty queen she is, she comes out of the bathroom, fully dressed and ready. I slip into my ankle boots and finish myself off with a spritz of my favorite perfume.

"Ready?" Alice turns to me and smiles.

"Ready," I confirm, and we both head out together.

The walk to Lincoln Hall is short, and we make it there in

under ten minutes. The building itself looks older than dirt, but inside it's beautiful, with high ceilings and huge windows that let lots of light in. Entering the room, I discover it's already filling up with people. There is an entrance table with one of the helpers handing out name tags and explaining the seating chart. Great, I won't be able to sit with Alice like I had hoped. A nervous knot forms in my stomach. That's just the way the cookie crumbles, Willow. Sighing, I walk up to the table.

"Willow Bradford," I tell the lady at the table.

"Good morning, Miss Bradford, you will be sitting at table eight, and your father is already here," she smiles, and I almost choke on the air in my lungs.

"What?" I don't understand. He's not supposed to be here. Why is he here? Suddenly any appetite I might have had is gone, and all I want to do is go back to the dorm and crawl in my bed. But I can't, definitely not now. Scanning the room slowly half praying this woman might be wrong, I spot him. *Damnit.* My insides burn, and my muscles tighten. There he is sitting at our assigned table, wearing a gray tailored suit looking every bit out of his element. His dark gaze moves about the room, watching as students pass by with their parents. Parents that care. That love them. As I stare, one single question remains. *What the hell is he doing here?*

"Oh, cool. Your dad came, after all," Alice exclaims excitedly. "My family is at table 3, but we can get together later, okay?" She's bubbling at the seams with excitement over seeing her parents, while I would rather stick forks in my eyes. I swallow thickly, the saliva in my mouth suddenly turning to glue. Not wanting to have to explain to her the shitshow that is my family, I just nod instead.

We part ways, and it takes everything inside me to continue walking toward that table. I'm angry, sad, and disappointed because this was supposed to be my break. My chance at freedom, instead, it feels more like a gilded cage. All over again, I'm trapped, just like I was at home.

"There you are," my father greets me with a forced smile as I walk up to the table. He gets up, presses a kiss to my cheek, and pulls my chair out for me. Once we're both seated, he leans in so no one else can hear and says, "Would it have killed you to wear a dress for an event like this?"

What the hell?

He straightens back up, and I stare at him dumbfoundedly. What has gotten into him? Why is this stupid brunch so important to him, and what is wrong with the clothes I'm wearing? This isn't a charity ball or some fundraiser. Everyone else is dressed in a similar fashion to me.

Biting back a shitty remark, I ignore his comment about my attire and decide to change the topic, "Why are you here?"

His thick eyebrows shoot up his forehead. "What kind of question is that? Why wouldn't I be here? All the other freshmen parents are here." As he is talking, his eyes scope out the room, almost like he is looking for *something... no... someone.*

Suspicion creeps up my spine and starts to fester deep inside my gut as I continue watching my dad. Even though he's supposedly here for me, his attention is everywhere but on me. Matter of fact, he almost seems distracted. I'm not really shocked though. Crossing my arms over my chest, I just stare at him, wishing he would disappear.

"Have you made a lot of friends yet?" he asks out of the blue.

"I really haven't had much time. I spent the last few days getting oriented with the campus and unpacking. My roommate is nice though. She wants to meet you later, but you don't have to."

"*Nice?*" he asks like he doesn't know what the word means. "What's her name?"

"Alice," I answer briskly, before taking a sip of my water.

He looks at me like I'm dumb. "What's her *last* name, Willow."

I'm so close to rolling my eyes, it's not even funny. Of course, he's only interested in her last name. Because last names signify everything about you. Forget what kind of person you are. Without the right last name, you're a nobody.

I shrug. "I don't know. Burton, I think."

"Burton?" My father rubs at his chin as if he's deep in thought, "Hmmm, doesn't ring a bell, which means she doesn't matter. You need to make some more friends. More *important* friends. Remember, it isn't *what* you know, it's *who* you know, that will get you places. This is the perfect school for you to make those kinds of friends, so don't waste this opportunity. You aren't here to make lifelong friends. You're here to make connections, Willow."

Curling my fingers into my hand, I sink my nails into the tender flesh of my palm. Of course, he is here for his own gain. Disappointment sinks like a heavy stone to the bottom of my stomach.

"You didn't drive two hours one way just to tell me that, did you? Because if you did, you're going to be gravely disappointed. I'm not here to make connections or friends. I'm just here because it was this or home with you, and anything is better than being stuck in that mansion with you." I'm talking out of line, antagonizing him, but I don't care. All I want is for him to feel even a sliver of the same pain my sister or me feel.

Raging fire flickers in his dark eyes, his jaw tenses, "You promised you wouldn't make a mockery out of me, Willow. And part of that is you needing to represent me and our family name in an elegant manner. So whether you like it or not, you *will* befriend people of importance, you *will* wear clothes that are appropriate, and you *will* do all of those things with a smile on your face, or do I need to remind you of what happens if you don't?"

I open my mouth to speak, to reply with anything, but I'm interrupted before I can.

"Welcome, dear students and families," a female voice filters through the speakers. "We are so happy to have you all here today..." she continues her speech, but I drown the rest of it out. All I can think about is my father's threats, his demands, and what happens to my poor sister if I don't comply. I hate him, truly, I do.

Gritting my teeth, I sit through the rest of the brunch, which thankfully goes by in a blur. After we are done eating, everyone gets up to mingle, which is exactly what my father came here for. I consider leaving right then and there, just to spite my father, but I won't pay for it. My sister will, and I can't let an innocent pay the price for my wrongdoings.

Alice finds us first; her parents greet us with smiles and friendliness, while my father looks them up and down like they are wearing dirty rags. Great, he's going to cost me my only friend.

"Burton, is it?" My father tsks, and I already know where this is going to go. "I don't think I've heard that name before."

"Yes, Burton," Alice's father replies while shaking my father's hand. Like most men, he doesn't seem even a little intimidated by my father. "I try to keep my name out of the spotlight as much as I can. I'm more of a silent partner."

My father smiles, but it looks more like if a shark smiled at you. His eyes light up, and excitement overtakes his features. Of course, that piques his interest. It doesn't matter where we are or what we're doing. Business is the only thing that matters to him. My father's conversation carries on while Alice and her mom excuse themselves to go and talk to someone else they know. Pretending I don't care, I smile and cross my arms over my chest. It's almost too hard to watch as all the happy families laugh and hug. I won't ever have this, a happy family, someone that is excited to see me. Ugh, pity party for one, I guess. Distracting myself, my gaze wanders around the room until I find a person in the far corner of the room...

He's half cloaked in darkness, the shadows covering his face. Even without seeing his features, I feel like I know him. The way he holds his body, there is something so familiar about it. I rack my brain, trying to recall meeting someone such as him, but nothing comes. Right then, the small hairs on the back of my neck rise up, goosebumps spread across my arms, and my heart starts to beat in an irregular rhythm. Dread fills my gut, and even though I have no reason to feel the way that I do right now, I can't shut the feelings off. It's like deep down, I know something bad is going to happen.

What is going on?

Like a hand gripping onto your leg in an old horror movie, fear claws at me, threatening to pull me under. I can't even see his face, only the contours of his broad shoulders, muscular chest, and the way his large hand is wrapped around the delicate glass he's holding. It's almost as if with the simplest of pressures, he could break it.

He could break me. I shake the thought away, unsure where it came from to begin with. I don't know him, whoever he is.

I'm about to turn to let my father know that I'm leaving when someone, *no,* not someone, a man comes to stand in front of me. My eyes lift to his face, he can't be but a little older than me. He's handsome in a my-father-is-rich-as-sin kind of way. Perfectly tailored clothes, meticulously styled hair, and a sharp jawline.

He smiles at me, showing off his dimples and a set of straight and sparkling white teeth. His eyes twinkle with mischievous, the color of deliciously melted chocolate.

"I'm pretty sure I'd remember meeting a pretty face like yours. You must be one of the freshmen?"

I smile as well because his smile is infectious, "Well, this is the freshman brunch, isn't it?" I cringe at the words after they've already come out.

Mystery man gives me a low chuckle, it's deep, and I can feel it in my bones, "I mean, yeah, but I'm not a freshman, and I'm here too, so ..." His eyes glitter with amusement.

"Sorry, that was rude of me," I apologize half-heartedly.

He nods, takes a sip of his drink, and for a split second, I let my gaze roam over him. Muscular chest, broad shoulders, big hands. He's tall, much taller than me, towering over me by a good four inches. He's got the body of an athlete, but somehow, I doubt he plays sports.

"Like what you see?" he says coyly.

My cheeks burn. "I wasn't checking you out. I was just..." *Shit, what was I doing?*

"It's okay if you were. I was checking you out too, and in case you were wondering..." He leans into my face, and as I suck a panicked breath into my lungs, I catch a whiff of his cologne. Sandalwood and patchouli. Warm, rich, and inviting. "I like what I've seen thus far." He winks, and while his demeanor is playful, I can't help but feel like there is a deeper meaning to what he is saying. *I like what I've seen thus far.* Like he'll have the chance to see more.

"Willow..." My father's deep baritone voice catches my ears, and I blink, pulled from my thoughts. Twisting around, I meet his hard gaze.

"Yes," I answer even though I don't want to.

"I'll let you get back to spending some time with your family. I'll see you around, Willow, is it?"

"Yes, Willow," I force my lips into a smile and extend my hand out to him. He takes it, his warm hand encompassing mine, as he gives it a gentle squeeze.

"Warren," he introduces himself, a boyish grin on his lips. *Warren.* The name seems to fit him. Prim and proper. "I'm sure I'll see your beautiful face around."

I nod, caught up in his words. Lifting my hand, he presses a kiss to the top before releasing it. It falls back down to my side as he turns and disappears into the crowded room like an illusion. *Weird.*

My father turns to where I had been looking, a moment ago. For a few seconds, he seems pleased with me, but we all know he can't have that.

"Did you ask for his last name?"

I snort, "No, father, I did not." I grind my teeth together so hard my jaw aches.

"Quit being difficult and just do what I've asked of you. I need at least one of my daughters to live up to the family name. Your sister has already disappointed me. Don't do the same. I can only handle one family fuck up at a time."

Turning to face him, I bare my teeth. *How dare he!*

"Ashton is not and never will be a disappointment," I speak through my teeth, finally having reached my limit with his bullshit. *You are the fuck up*, I add in my head.

He takes a threatening step toward me, and I try not to react to the closeness; he is, after all, my father. I shouldn't be afraid of him, but I'm not that naive. He's not only rich but also powerful, even without all the *friends* he's lost over the last two years. If I get in his way, he'll squish me like a bug, daughter or not.

"Your sister cost me everything. She is more than a disappointment, and if you don't fall in line with how I want things to be, then I'll have no reason to keep supporting her. I'm doing this for you, and only you."

Tears sting my eyes, threatening to spill over. "She's your daughter," I croak. How can he be so heartless toward his own child?

Darkness glitters his eyes, there is no remorse, not a single shred of compassion. If I didn't know it before, I am certain now that my father is nothing more than a heartless monster.

"She's nothing, and you will be nothing if you don't learn to follow my orders. Do as you're told, Willow. Don't ask questions. Obey me, and you and your disappointment of a sister will be just fine."

Swallowing around the lump of fear that's lodged in my throat, I nod. There isn't any point in speaking anyway. Not to him, not to a person who doesn't care about anything besides himself. I was so naive to think that by coming here I would be safe. I should have known that his corruption and power would be able to reach me anywhere... I should've known better.

"Make a mockery out of me a second time, and I'll make sure you never see or hear from Ashton again." He turns, letting the threat linger in the air between us as I stand there. I'm in a sea of people but couldn't feel any more alone.

2

PARKER

*R*evenge. It consumes me. It's the pillar of life. The hate for Willow and her sister has become my newest obsession and will be my biggest downfall. It's been festering inside of me for years, eating away at me like a cancer, but today it's reached an all-new level. Seeing her for the first time in two years. It's like an indescribable high.

I didn't believe my father when he told me she would be coming here. As sick and twisted as it is, part of me hoped it wasn't true, while the other craved for it to be. Craved to have her near, so I could punish her for what she did. I curl my fingers into my hands, the thought of being close enough to touch her has me on edge.

Watching her the last couple of days has been both torture and exciting. My fingers itch to touch her. To mark her. I want to run my hands across her porcelain skin just to see if it's as soft and smooth as it looks. I want to inhale her sweet scent into my lungs and let it drag me under. *No.* I snarl to myself.

I can't get distracted by her beauty. I need to concentrate on what I really want...really *need*. I remind myself that her beauty is only an illusion, hiding the ugly person inside. Everything about Willow is a facade, she's faker than most of the girls here at Blackthorn.

Trying my best to blend in and not raise any attention, I stay in the background. Hiding my face in the few shadowy corners, this large room has to offer. I'm not used to this, hiding in plain sight. Normally, I would be the center of attention, the spotlight on me, but not today. I don't think most people here even know who I am, not yet anyway.

As I watch from across the room, my eyes move from Willow to her father, William Bradford. He's talking to another parent, doesn't care about anything but money and power. I'll bet anything his daughter being here has very little to do with getting a good education and everything to do with getting back in the good graces of the elite families. I still wonder how he got her enrolled in the first place. Why did my father let her attend?

"Dude, what the hell is wrong with you?" Warren, one of my best friends, says, as he nudges me in the arm.

"Nothing," I grit out, but my response doesn't match my behavior. There's loads wrong with me, and Warren can see that from a mile away.

"Is that her?" he asks, tipping the champagne flute in his hand toward her.

All I do is grunt because she's not worthy of any more of my attention, let alone both of ours. Warren follows my line of vision, and we both stare at her as she scowls at all the other families as they pass by. Does she think she is better than everybody here? Probably.

"She's pretty, in a Snow White kind of way." He isn't wrong. Black hair, ivory skin, and ruby red lips. She does look like Snow White, and I guess that makes me her Huntsman. The only difference is, our story won't end like a fairytale.

"Don't be fooled by her beauty, it's just a trick, an illusion to hide all the ugly on the inside. She might be pretty, but she's like a deadly poison."

"All women are like poison," he mumbles, his face scrunching up as he stares at her more intently. Gritting my teeth, I stop myself from slugging him in the face. I have to remind myself that he is not the enemy here, she is.

My obsession with her has ruled my mind for so long. It's hard for me to shove the territorial thoughts away, to separate me wanting to have her and wanting to destroy her. She's not mine, and she never will be.

"What's the plan?"

"Revenge. I will make her life a living hell while she is here. I'm going to make her feel the same pain she caused my family." *And then some.*

"You mean to tell me you aren't going to sample that fine piece of ass before you destroy her? Or maybe that's how you get your revenge? What if she's a virgin? Wouldn't that be the perfect way to make her pay? To claim the one and only thing she has to give her new husband?"

My throat tightens, and I swallow thickly at the thought. For years I've wondered what it would be like to dive between her thighs and taste her. To drink from her until there was nothing left. Would I feast, ravishing her, or would I sip like a fine wine?

"This isn't the fifteen hundreds. She is eighteen, I highly doubt she is still a virgin or saving herself for marriage."

Warren cocks his head to the side, and out of the corner of my eye, I see his gaze raking over her body. Across the room, unaware of all the attention, she stands with her arms crossed over her chest. The swell of her breasts is peeking out of that innocent-looking pink blouse, and I wonder if she knows that she is pushing up her tits standing like that.

My eyes move on their own, traveling over her heart-shaped face, and those sparkling green eyes, that hold a million and one secrets. I burn to crack her open, to snap her in two, and see what comes out.

"Maybe, or maybe not? You never know, and with as cold and uptight as she looks, I wouldn't be surprised. She seems like she needs to be thoroughly fucked."

"Shut up," I growl, tugging the hood of my sweater further down over my face. "I doubt it, and even if she is, I don't care. It changes nothing." I have a different idea on how to break her.

Warren smirks. "Well, if you don't care, I think I'll just waltz on over there and introduce myself. Test the waters a little? Get my dick wet? You know I'm all about leaving a lasting impression." The fucker winks, and I curl my hand into a tight fist instinctively. Best friend or not, I would punch him in the face without thought.

Asshole. I bite my tongue, feeling compelled to tell him, no, but I don't. Willow is free game to any fuckface at this school, Warren included.

"Be my guest, but I don't want to hear you bitching when you catch something. You don't know who has been between her legs."

"I'll look at it before I stick my dick in it. Make sure there is no rash," he snickers. "Or at least, not a nasty looking one."

"Good luck with that." He's probably going to be the one to give her something. I make a habit of not fucking girls after Warren has been with them, which narrows down the list of available pussy dramatically. "Let me know how *experienced* she was when you are done."

"Doesn't matter. After I've been there, all the others will be a forgotten memory." Flipping me his middle finger, he walks away and heads for her like a cat prowling across the African savanna. She'll never stand a chance against Warren. He's a natural predator, even worse than me. Curiously, I watch as he greets her. Like most women, she smiles as he introduces himself.

Everything inside of me says to follow him over there, to drag him away, but I can't. I don't want to give myself away yet. The element of surprise is going to be my biggest asset here. Willow will never see me coming, and that's what I need. I can't wait to see her face fill with fear when she realizes she's walked head-first into her own nightmare.

As I'm standing there, watching; Willow smiles at something Warren says, a wave of jealousy slams into me. It's powerful enough to take me out at the knees, but I suck in a deep breath and push it down, burying it deep inside my gut.

Fucking asshole.

Shaking my head, I tell myself that I'm not going to let Warren ruin this for me. Not with his antics, charm, or snide comments. And Willow, she's not worth being jealous over. I can have any girl I want here at Blackthorn. She's nothing special. Nothing at all.

Lost in thought for a brief moment, I miss the rest of the interaction between Warren and Willow, and when I look back up, I find Willow cowering beneath her father's icy gaze. I don't know why, but in that moment, I want to walk over there and kick her father's ass. I want to tell him that he doesn't belong here, that the only person that can hurt her is me, but I don't. Instead, I tamp down the feeling, reminiscing about all the wrongs the Bradfords have done to my family.

"Breaking her is going to be so easy. She's delicate, like glass, when I kissed her hand, I swear, she shivered." I can see the wheels in Warren's head turning. "I will definitely help you break her. It'll be fun, give me something to do." He wiggles his eyebrows, "And I do mean literally. She's prettier than I expected. I might give her a ride or two."

Snapping, I growl, "Her beauty has nothing to do with this."

Warren snickers, "Liar. It has everything to do with it. Her beauty is a weakness for you."

Taking a step toward Warren, I bump my chest into his.

We're the same height, same body type. In a fight, we would be pretty much equal, that is, if he'd ever fight. I doubt he's ever fought in his life. I might come from a filthy rich family, but I've gotten my hands dirty more than once. Warren is nothing more than a pretty boy with a sick and twisted mind. He's a fly, a gnat. I don't know why, but I feel the need to remind him that she's mine. That all of this has to do with my revenge on her.

Gritting my teeth, I stare down my best friend. "She's mine to break. Mine to hurt. Do you understand that, or do I need to explain it to you in detail?" My fists clench and unclench, rage flickering through my veins like an out of control forest fire.

Warren blinks, and for a moment, it looks like he's going to fight me on it, but instead, he gives me a chin nod and takes a step back. *That's right, you know you don't stand a chance.* A sickening satisfaction fills my gut. Not wanting to make a scene, I back down. I have better things to do for the rest of the day.

Tonight, I'll make my presence known.

Tonight, I'll remind her of all the wrong her family has done.

3

WILLOW

The wind chills me to the bone as I walk across campus back to my dorm. The fall night air is crisp, and the stars blanket the sky like a million twinkling lights. Wrapping my arms around myself, I wish that Alice had decided to come back to the room with me.

After brunch with my father and a run-in with one of the many rich boys of Blackthorn, I spent the rest of the day with Alice and her parents. We went bowling and then did some shopping before having dinner together. Almost like *gasp* a family.

They offered me a ride back to the dorms, but I refused. I feel bad as it is for having crashed their family fun. Plus, the walk from the cocktail bar they went to isn't far. The place is five minutes away from the campus edge, the perfect location for students.

As the dorms come into sight, a chill ripples through me, but it isn't from the cold. No, this chill is the kind you feel deep in your gut, the kind that makes the small hairs on the back of your neck stand up. Fear creeps up my spine like a thousand little bugs crawling under my skin.

Reaching into my purse, my fingers shake as I fish out the key card to open the front door. When I finally get to the entrance and manage to pull the damn card out, I swipe it in a rush. The tiny red light blinks, and I groan into the air. *Seriously?*

I slide the card again, still nothing. My pulse is racing, and even though I'm cold, there is sweat forming on my brows and hands. Glancing over my shoulder, I quickly scan the area. I don't see anyone, but I still feel like someone is watching me.

It's almost like I'm in one of those ridiculous horror movies, hiding, waiting for the monster to find me. Forcing air into my lungs, I tell myself to calm down. *You're safe. No one here knows you. No one knows what you did.* After sliding the card a third time, the green light finally blinks. A clicking noise comes from the lock, and I'm able to push the door open the next second. Warm air blows against my face as I enter, and once I'm inside, I pull the door shut behind me. Standing there for a moment, I sigh in relief and almost slump against the door.

What the hell was that? I must be going crazy. Looking through the glass door, I stare at the wooded area across the street, waiting, watching for something to happen. But after a few minutes, nothing appears, and I'm left wondering if I've lost my mind.

I'm alone. No one is out there.

Shaking my head and the irrational fear away, I turn around and walk up the single flight of stairs to my room. The dorm is unusually quiet tonight, but I guess that's to be expected. Classes will be starting soon, and most of the students are visiting with their families. Exchanging the tiny ass dorm bed for a decent sized one.

Using the same card I used to open the front door downstairs, I place it in the slot beside the doorknob of my dorm and listen as the lock disengages on the first try. The door creaks as

I push it open and step across the threshold. Reaching for the light switch, I take another step.

My fingers graze the very edge of the switch, but before I can flip it on, someone grabs me from behind. Everything happens so fast I can barely comprehend what's going on. Before I can even think of crying out for help, a hand comes slamming down over my mouth. A scream catches in my throat, only to come out as a muffled whimper when I'm shoved against the nearest wall face first. I can't breathe. I can't do anything. My attacker kicks the door shut next, ruining any chance of someone seeing us, or me seeing his face.

My eyes are wide open, but with the room draped in complete darkness, I can't even see a foot in front of me. The smell of whiskey and soap tickles my nostrils as I suck in a precious breath of oxygen. Without warning, I'm gripped by the shoulder, my attacker's fingers dig into my skin with just enough pressure to cause pain, and I'm flipped around, my back meeting the wall a second later, and the hand is removed from my mouth.

Opening my mouth to speak, I find I can't form a single word, my tongue heavy in my mouth. My pulse pounds loudly in my ears, banging like a drum.

Thump. Thump. Thump.

I just stand there, petrified with fear. My arms hanging down at my sides, useless limbs.

The same fingers from my shoulder, start trailing down between my breasts. *What's going to happen?* I'm shaking now, my entire body vibrating.

I can't just stand here, I have to do something, anything...

"I..." My lips wobble, a sob building in my throat.

"Shut up!" The sound is violent, dark, deep, angry, so angry. His words pulse through me like a second heartbeat, and I don't understand why I just stand there. Why don't I try and fight him? With his other hand, he circles my throat, gently squeezing the flesh as if he's testing its durability. The pressure against my throat makes it hard for me to focus on anything else. Is he going to strangle me? Hurt me? His touch is firm, warm, and I gasp when I feel his nose skim against my cheek.

He inhales through his nose, and it's almost as if he's smelling me. He squeezes, and I lift my hands, grabbing at his hand around my throat. There's no point in fighting him though. Like an annoying fly, he swats them away, and instead squeezes harder, warning me, proving that he holds all the power. Letting my hands fall away, I do my best not to struggle as my lungs burn with the need for air. Slowly, his grip eases, and breathing comes easier, each labored breath making my breasts brush against his solid chest.

Seconds tick by, but I remain still, my body rippling with fear. My throat throbs and my knees threaten to give out on me, but somehow, I still manage to keep myself standing up.

"I've been watching you, Willow," he finally speaks; his tone a little more collected now. "I've been watching you since you got to campus. I haven't seen you in so long. So long, I almost forgot how sweet you smelled."

Through the fog of fear, I notice that his voice sounds vaguely familiar to me, something about it tugs at my memory, but I can't place it. Can't connect a face to the dark sound of his voice.

"Who..." I croak, only to have the word cut off by the tightening of his grip once more.

"I said, shut up!" He growls into my face, his hot breath fanning against my cheeks. He gives me a hard shove against the wall, and my head bounces off of it like a basketball.

"That's always been your problem. You just couldn't shut up. You couldn't keep your nose in your own business. If you had just kept your mouth shut and stopped the lies from pouring out, we wouldn't be here right now. I wouldn't be here to make you pay for what you did to my brother." Like a bucket of cold water raining down on me, I piece the broken puzzle pieces together in my mind.

"P-Parker?" I say his name in a whisper, praying that I'm wrong. Hoping that I'm wrong.

"The one and only." Even wrapped in the darkness of the room, I still know he's smiling. I can feel it on my skin. My breathing turns erratic in a second, and the panic bubbles up inside me. How did he find me? How did he know I would be here?

"Please, don't. I didn't..." My mouth clamps shut when his fingers grip on to my chin with bruising force, a low whimper the only thing that escapes me.

"Like a lamb walking into the lion's den, you practically offered yourself to me by showing up here." *No. Oh, god.* I try and shake from his hold, try and break free, but his hands are like shackles, and I'm too afraid to fight him further, afraid that he, too, might hurt me. "Did you think I would show you mercy simply because you have a nice pair of tits and ass?"

He chuckles, but there isn't any humor in his words.

"Please, let me go. I didn't do anything wrong." It's hard to speak with his fingers digging into my cheeks, but somehow, I get the words out.

"Oh, sweet, Willow," he taunts. "You still won't admit that you lied, and that's the problem here. No one has taught you a lesson. No one has put the princess in her place, but that's about to change." I can feel him moving, his lips press against my throbbing pulse. It's as tender of a touch as it is terrifying. A low groan fills the room, and the sound zings straight through me, sending rivulets of pleasure into my core.

No. This is wrong.

"You know, the worst part is that I thought you were different," he whispers against my skin. "I thought better of you...but you really showed me, didn't you? You made me believe in something that could never be. I thought you were a good girl. I was wrong, terribly wrong." I gasp as his teeth rake across my flesh.

"I..." Is all I can get out. Even without his hand around my throat, I don't think I could speak right now. I'm too overwhelmed with emotions.

"This is your one warning. Stay here, and I will rip you apart, piece by piece. I will take and take until there is nothing left to take, just as you and your sister did to my family. To my brother." I shake my head without even realizing it. His family is the one who wronged mine. His brother is the one who hurt my sister, who destroyed our lives.

This can't be happening right now. This can't be the way things are going to be. I did the right thing. I know I did, but right in this moment, it feels like all I've done is sign my own death certificate.

There is no peace, no forgetting what happened that night.

"You have to help me, Willow. You have too." My sister sobs, her entire body shaking, and all I can do is stand there and watch because I don't understand. I don't know what to do. I don't know how to fix what happened.

"How?" I croak, wanting so badly to take my sister's pain away. I haven't felt this broken or lost since Mom died, leaving my sister and me behind to fend for ourselves against our father.

Ashton looks up at me, her eyes are rimmed red and tears stain her cheeks, "Tell them. Tell everyone. Be my voice, please, Willow. I'm begging you."

With a gasp, I'm pulled from the memory and placed back in the present. Parker still has me by the neck, I'm nothing more than his unwilling victim. Acid burns up my throat, and my stomach churns. I think I'm going to be sick.

"Leave. Never come back. Never show your face here again, and I'll consider not hurting you." There is a brief pause, and I wonder what more he could possibly say, but then he clears his throat and starts to speak again, "But stay, and I'll make sure you wish you'd never met me. From here on out, I'll be your biggest nightmare. Hope you aren't afraid of the dark."

And just like that, he releases me. Like I'm fire, and he's gasoline. Like one more touch could push him over the edge. Gasping, I almost fall to the floor, not even realizing how much of his body was holding my own up.

Squeezing my eyes shut, I slide down the wall until my ass meets the floor. When I hear the click of the door opening and then closing, I let out a ragged breath, followed by an uncontrolled sob. I bite my bottom lip, holding in the scream that wants to rip from my throat. How could I have been so stupid?

He's here. Tears well in my eyes. Shame. Anger. Pain. It all resides inside of me, swirling around and around. The boy I once knew is here. But he's not the same. Now he wants to hurt me. Now he wants to destroy me, and if I'm not careful, he'll do just that.

I have to escape. I have to leave. But how?

∼

OPENING my eyes the next morning, the first thing I do is touch the tender skin around my neck. It's almost like I can still feel him there, still feel his fingers curled around my throat. Each finger imprinted on my skin. Branding me.

Sitting up slowly, I realize it's already bright outside, the sun peeking through the curtains. Checking my phone, I see that it's past nine. I usually don't sleep this long, but I barely slept last night, so I'm not too surprised. Matter of fact, I feel like I haven't slept at all. My muscles ache, my stomach is nothing more than a ball of knots.

All over again, I'm back to feeling anxious, terrified of what's to come.

My gaze flicks to Alice, who is quietly snoring across the room. She's sleeping soundly, peacefully, and I'm jealous of that because I know it'll be a long time before I can sleep like that again. For a long time, I just sit there on my bed, trying to figure out what to do. Every thought leads me down a dead-end road.

My father will not be okay with me leaving, even with Parker here, even with him threatening me. He'll simply tell me to stand my ground. To grow a backbone. He'll say I brought this on myself. I know it. But I have to do something. My hands shake, and panic grips on to me, refusing to let go. I don't feel safe here. I don't feel anything but anger and fear. Breathing deeply, I tell myself that I can't just let him break into my room and treat me like this. I have to do something. Anything.

Trying not to be loud, so I don't wake Alice, I slip out of the bed and tiptoe into the bathroom. Closing the door behind me, I flick on the light. While brushing my teeth, I take a closer look in the mirror. I look sickly, my skin is ashen, my eyes lifeless. There are dark circles under them, and as I stare at my reflection, I'm surprised to find no bruises around my neck. I don't bruise easily, but yesterday, I was sure he'd leave marks. It felt like he was strangling me. Or maybe that was just the fear of it all.

The memory of him in this room with me makes my skin crawl. When we were kids, Parker was always kind to me. At first, we had only come to know each other in passing, but as time went on and we got older, I started to see him more, at social gatherings, the country club, at meetings between our parents.

I try not to picture him as that kind boy, but instead as the one who threatened me last night. Those two are very different people, and it's impossible to believe that they can live inside the same person.

Sneaking back into the bedroom, I get dressed as swiftly as I can, before sneaking out quietly. Walking through the dorms, my eyes flicker to every corner, every noise, almost as if I'm expecting Parker to jump out and attack me. He did this to me.

The walk across campus isn't much better. My heart is in my throat the entire time, and I'm unable to shake the constant fear looming right beneath my skin, threatening to swallow me whole. Like a lunatic, I look around. I feel like I'm being watched, all eyes on me as I walk into the campus security office.

God, I hate him. I hate him so much.

"Hello, Miss, what can we do for you today?" One of the two officers sitting inside the office greets me. He is a pudgy middle-aged guy, his hair graying, but he has a friendly smile, so that eases me a little.

"Hi, ah… I want to report an incident," I say, my voice a little unsure. Only in this moment do I realize that I'm going to have to tell them the whole story. Tell them in detail what happened last night. Relive the whole thing.

A grain of doubt is planted in my gut, spreading quickly like weeds overflowing a garden. Am I ready for this? Ready to do this? Memories of the investigation around my sister resurface. Memories I've been trying to forget for so long. How I was interrogated that night. How scared and helpless I felt.

"I'm sorry to hear that, please come in and have a seat," the other officer waves me forward. He is younger, maybe early thirties. His hair is cut short, and his face is shaved clean, giving him more of a police officer look than the other guy.

Walking further into the room, I take a seat at one of the desks. Both of the officers take a seat across from me. I stare down at my trembling hands wishing they would stop.

"I'm Officer Walden," the older guy introduces himself, "and this is my partner, Officer Healy," he points to the younger guy.

"I'm Willow. Willow Bradford," I introduce myself.

"Miss Bradford, can you tell us exactly what happened? Start from the beginning."

He flips open a laptop that I hadn't noticed was sitting on the table and starts typing, though his eyes never waver from mine. At the same time, Officer Healy gets out a notepad and pencil and writes something down.

I start from the beginning, recounting every last detail. The officers nod and continue taking all my information as I talk. As I speak of the incident inside the bedroom, one of the officers interrupts me.

"Do you know this person? The man that attacked you?"

I nod, my throat tightening. Deep down, I'm not sure I have anything to be scared of when it comes to Parker. Yes, he's vicious, and he terrified me last night, but it was nothing more than a bully tactic. He made threats, but he didn't actually hurt me. Not like he could've. Not like I know he wanted to.

"Who is he?"

My lips tremble, "Parker Rothschild."

As soon as his name has fallen from my lips, both officers freeze. Officer Healy stops writing mid-word, putting the pencil down on the desk. Officer Walden stops typing, his fingers hovering over the keyboard unmoving. They both glance at each other, some silent conversation happening between them before Healy returns his attention back to me.

"Are you sure this is who you saw? You said it was dark."

"Yes, I'm positive. I know Parker, I've known him and his family for years. It was him. I know it was him."

"Mhm..." Walden rubs his chin as if he is thinking about how to get rid of me, while his colleague rips the page he has been writing on from his notebook and starts ripping it up.

What the hell?

"I don't think we'll be able to help you with this, Miss Bradford. You said it yourself, it was dark and no one else was there.

Who is to say you didn't make the whole thing up? You don't even have any bruises."

With my mouth hanging open, I sit there staring at them, dumbfounded. Is this happening, or is this just part of the nightmare? Maybe I'm still asleep, unable to wake up.

"I think it's in your best interest if you just forget about the whole thing."

I rear back as if he's slapped me. "In *my* best interest?"

"Best for everybody, you included. Don't make this hard on yourself. Just let it go."

Just let it go? What is wrong with these people? I just told them I was attacked in my room, and they tell me to let it go?

"Now if you would excuse us, we have some work to finish up," he dismisses me like I've been nothing more than wasting his time.

I want to cry. I want to cry so badly, but I won't, not here. Rubbing at the corner of my eye to hide the tears, I stare at the two men.

"You have to help me. Someone has to help me. How am I supposed to be safe at the dorms? How am I supposed to sleep at night knowing he can walk in whenever he wants to? This is wrong, and you both know it." My voice cracks, and it feels like something inside me does too. Like I'm breaking, fracturing down the middle.

"We can't help you. Now, please leave, Miss Bradford," Officer Healy orders, and for half a second, all I can do is sit there staring hopelessly at the two *officers*. How is this possible? How can he get away with this? He isn't god, he doesn't own this school, but the officers are acting like he does.

Without another word, I get up and shuffle out of the room, my feet gliding across the floor as I force myself out of the office.

Fear and disappointment reside deep in my gut, but so does anger. It burns through me, and with clenched fists, I march back to my dorm. I hold on to that anger and let it drive me. If the officers can't or won't help me, then I'll have to find a way to help myself. I'm not my sister. I'm not weak.

If Parker wants me to leave, he's going to have to do more than scare me.

4

PARKER

Walking into advanced American literature, I peer around the room to see who is here that I know. One sweep of the area and all I find are some girls who look vaguely familiar. They bat their eyelashes, and on autopilot, I smile at them. *Not going there.*

Grumbling under my breath, I rake a hand through my black hair and take a seat in the back of the room, hoping none of those chicks decide to get up and follow me. All they're going to do is get on my nerves, making this already long class, longer.

Over the course of a few minutes, the room starts to fill, more and more fellow Blackthorn students walk in. Before I know it, the only open seat left is the one next to me. When the professor finally starts talking, thank fuck, the seat remains empty, I sigh, sagging down into my chair.

Opening my notebook, I grab a pen and prepare myself for a ninety-minute lecture.

"Everyone open your books and take a look at chapter two, so we can—" The professor is interrupted by the creaking of the door. All heads lift, including my own, to see who the hell is walking in, late for the class.

"I'm so sorry, I couldn't find the building," Willow apologizes, stepping over the threshold and into the classroom. Even across the room, I can feel her. The pull she has on me. It's magnetic, sinister. Being near her is like sticking my finger into a light socket. It thrills me, excites me, but at the same time is dangerous.

I wasn't sure if she'd left after I cornered her in her room. Part of me hoped she would, but the other part... a much larger part hoped she would still be here.

"I'll give you a pass since it's the first day, but don't let it happen again," Professor Wade warns. Willow nods as she looks up, and into the crowd, most likely trying to find a seat. Her eyes scan the classroom and land on me half a second later. Even from across the room, I can see her swallow thickly, and I can't help but grin, amused by the way I make her uncomfortable. *Good, fear me. It's better than the alternative.*

Two crimson splotches appear on her cheeks, and I wonder if it's because she's embarrassed or if it's because she's realized that she has no choice but to sit beside me. Is she scared? Curious? I'm half expecting her to turn around and run out of the room, but to my surprise, she does the opposite. She walks to the back of the room with her head held high, a mask sliding on her face.

Oh, she wants to play that game? I can't help but grin, can't help but feel that distinct tingling in my gut, the one I used to get when I'd watch her, when I'd think about kissing her, deflowering her. She was my obsession, and now she would become my retribution.

Without ever making eye contact, she sits down next to me, gets her textbook out of her oversized designer purse, and opens it up. My jaw ticks as the seconds pass, and the temperature in the room spikes. *Jesus, is it fucking hot in here?* I can feel her body heat seeping into me, and we aren't even touching.

Her sweet scent fills my nostrils as I suck a labored breath into my lungs. She doesn't smell like all the other girls. Like high designer perfume that clings to every pore on your body. No, Willow smells divine like jasmine and vanilla. Pure. Naive. And all at once, I find the organ between my legs growing hard with need for the one person I shouldn't want. Teeth grinding together, I grip the pen in my hand hard enough to break it.

Why her? Why am I drawn to her? Why do I want her? I hate her as much as I want her, and I don't understand why. She's a liar, a fucking liar, and she cost my brother everything because she opened her mouth and spread lies. I bite back a growl, covering it with a cough. Professor Wade continues talking, but I don't hear a word he says. I can't think, focus, or even breathe with the lying temptress beside me.

When she shifts in her seat, I start to wonder if she's as uncomfortable as I am? Tick tock, tick tock. My arousal intertwines with the hate I have for her. A toxic mixture. I'm burning up with anger, and the longer I'm forced to stay within close quarters with her, the harder I get, and the more the hate pulses through me.

Wade dismisses us after what seems like an eternity in hell. The whole time I was sitting here, I thought I couldn't get away fast enough, but now that class is over, I don't want to leave. I want to see her scared again, wrap my fingers around her throat, feel her pulse beneath my touch. I want to hurt her.

"I thought you'd be gone by now," I tell her. "Figured I made myself clear with what would happen if you decided to stay."

"You don't scare me, Parker," she barks while gathering up her things and shoving them into her bag.

"Maybe not right this second, but you were the other night. You were trembling, probably close to pissing your pants," I taunt, wanting to lure her into the darkness. I stare down at her, at her throat, my gaze drops to the swell of her breasts that peek out of her shirt. They're big, perky, and I wonder what color her nipples are, a dusky pink like her cheeks were earlier?

Clenching my hands into fists, I dig my nails into my palms to stop myself from reaching out to her, to mark her.

"You know, I reported you to campus police," she blurts out, and I can't help but laugh, the sound echoing through the room.

"Did you now? I'm sure that went over well," I chuckle and shake my head. Such a stupid girl. Stupid, beautiful girl. Doesn't she know my father basically owns this school?

She swings her purse over her shoulder and turns to me. Her eyes lock with mine, a fire flickering deep inside of them, and all I want to do is stomp that fire out.

"They told me it didn't matter. That they couldn't help me." Her throat bobs as she swallows. *Not afraid, my ass.* "What kind of officer can't help a woman who was assaulted?" Those dark green eyes of hers pierce my heart, and for one single second, I see her as the girl she was before she pulled the rug out from underneath me. Before she destroyed me.

Leaning against the table, I shrug, "Personally, I would say a smart one. One that doesn't want to lose his job. And assaulted? Seriously? I didn't even hurt you." Not like I wanted to anyway.

Willow grits her teeth and takes a step toward me. If she's trying to intimidate me, it's not working. "Yes. You. Did. And you don't own this place, and you definitely don't own me. You can't just come into my room. You can't threaten me or try and hurt me. It's illegal, there are laws to protect me."

The balls of this girl. It's time I knock her down a peg or two. Lifting my hand, I bop her on the nose, "But I can, and I did. And no one here would dare cross me. Or my family. So, spoiler alert, there isn't anything you can do about it." I lean in a little closer, doing my best to intimidate her, "Why don't you do us both a favor and use that lying fucking mouth of yours for something other than speaking."

I look around the room, realizing that we've talked long enough for it to clear out. We are the only two people left. She follows my gaze, realizing the same.

I smirk, flicking the button on my jeans, I wait for her to start screaming, for the panic to set in, but instead, I find she's still standing here, a determined look painted on her features.

"I didn't lie," she snarls, and fuck, I'll be damned if that doesn't make my cock even harder. I wonder if she's ever given a blow job, hell, I wonder if I can go through with this. I guess we'll find out. Her anger mixes with my own, and it's like a nuclear battle is taking place inside me. Hurting her is going to be my next favorite past time.

"You did, you lied, and now my brother is paying the price." I speak through my teeth, "An innocent man's life is ruined and all because of you. Funny how one single lie can change an entire person's world."

Reaching into my pants, I pull my steel hard cock out. I'm not worried about anyone walking in. They'll turn around and walk out when they see what's happening, and if they don't, then I guess we'll give them a show.

Willow's green eyes widen, and her pink lips part at the sight of my length. An audible gasp fills the room, and the fact that it's come from her makes me wonder if this is her first time seeing a cock. The look on her face almost confirms my assumption. I can't stop my lips from curling into a sinister smile.

I'll break her. Take all her firsts. Ruin any future she ever had.

I'm done talking, nothing she says now will change what's happened.

"Have you ever given a blow job?" I reach for her with one

hand, pinching her chin between two fingers, while I use my other hand to stroke my cock.

She blinks, her mouth hanging open in shock and for a moment she just stares at me. Full-on stares, those big emerald eyes of hers bleed into mine. Time stands still for half a second, and it seems like I'm catching a glimpse into her soul.

Then, as if she's composed herself, she closes her mouth and straightens her spine. The shock and fear in her eyes morph into something different.

Determination? Lust? Is she turned on by this?

My suspicion is confirmed when she jerks from my hold and takes a tiny step toward me, closing the distance between us. Lifting her hand, she places it on my chest. Her touch burning into my skin through my shirt. I try my very best to keep my face blank, not to show any kind of emotion, but on the inside, I'm a fucking tornado wreaking havoc.

"A blow job, hmmm? That's what you want?" She lets her fingers trail down my chest, and I wonder if she can feel how fast my heart is beating. I can't believe she is fucking okay with this. I'm shocked, flabbergasted. I figured she would be running the other way as fast as she could. Now that she's making a move on me, I feel like the tables have turned.

Like I'm the prey, and she is the predator.

"Would you let me stay at this school with you if I suck your dick?"

"It would be a start," I shrug, as her hand trails down, and down, and when she looks up at me with them fuck me eyes, I swear, I nearly come unhinged.

"Okay…" She whispers, her fingers grazing my cock and the pre-cum that beads at the tip. For a split second, I close my eyes, giving in to the feeling, the desire. I've wanted this for so long. Every chick I've ever fucked, I've envisioned to be her, and now that something is happening, it's almost as if it's a dream.

With my defenses down, Willow takes that moment to pull

her hand away, and before I can open my eyes all the way to ask her if she's changed her mind, she jams her knee into my balls. The force of the blow sends me to my knees in an instant. Black spots form over my vision, and my stomach churns, acid rising up my throat.

Anger as hot as the fucking sun vibrates through my veins, and I grit my teeth, trying everything I can to push through the pain.

"Don't ever threaten me again, asshole. I'm not like everyone else, I'm not going to do what you want just because you say so. You can try to hurt me all you want, but I promise you, I won't break easily," she yells, and before I can get my tongue to work or my vision to focus on her, I hear her scampering out of the room.

"You bitch!" I slam my fist onto the ground, and seethe into the empty room, hoping maybe she has heard me. *Fuck.* She'll pay for this. I'm done. I'm not going to just scare her anymore. I'm going to be the nightmare she fucking knows I can be.

Run, Willow, run as fast as you can....

5

WILLOW

My feet pound against the pavement, the intensity of each step jarring my bones. *Oh, god. I shouldn't have done that. I really shouldn't have done it.* Air rushes into my lungs as I suck in a deep breath and sprint down the sidewalk and back to the dorm.

I know I'm not safe, not even there, but I do know one thing. Parker won't do anything in public. He isn't that stupid. But that doesn't mean he won't be able to come after me, find me in a dark corner of the campus, or just break into my room again.

I'm so screwed. I never should've let him get to me. All I did was feed right into his hate. I'm so disappointed in myself. Taking the steps two at a time, I run up them and down the hall, my key card already in hand. Sweat beads my brow as I swipe the thing with shaking fingers, surprised when it actually opens on the first try. *Thank God.*

Stepping inside quickly, I slam the door shut behind me and twist the lock into place before slumping against it. *Like some flimsy lock is going to protect me?* Pfft, I'm stupid. Black strands stick to my face, and when I hear a creak, I lift my eyes in the direction of the noise.

"What's wrong with you?" Alice's voice pierces through the air, and my already strained heart starts to thump out of rhythm again. Holding a hand against my chest, I press my palm to my sternum, as if my touch there could somehow calm the erratic beat.

"Sorry, I didn't see you there," I answer breathlessly.

Alice's brow furrows, and she frowns deeply, "Are you okay?"

"Yes... *no*, no, I'm not okay," I whine. Dragging my feet, I walk over to her bed and flop down next to her. "I'm so screwed, Alice. I really messed up this time."

Alice looks horror-stricken, "Oh, god, what happened? Did you sleep with someone's boyfriend? Hit on one of the hot, professors? Please say it was the second. I don't know that I could handle a scandal as big as—"

Interrupting her before she goes on a tirade, I say, "What? No! No, I didn't sleep with anyone's boyfriend or a teacher."

She visibly sighs, her eyes losing some of the surprise that mirrored in them, "Okay, spill the beans then. What did you do?"

Sucking in a panicked breath, I try and think about where I should start.

Peering down at me curiously, Alice waits while I try and catch my breath.

"Okay, so long story short, I know one of the other students that go here. Our families have known each other for years, and well, there is a lot of bad history between us." I continue but watch Alice's face with each word I speak. "The other night he threatened me, said some things that scared me. The next morning, I went to campus police, but they told me they couldn't do anything."

Her pink lips part and her mouth pops open, "Threatened how?"

"He told me I needed to leave, or he would make my life hell here."

"Wait, why? I don't understand. Am I missing something?"

I resist the urge to roll my eyes. None of this is Alice's fault. "He hates me... he hates my whole family, and truthfully, it's a long-ass story." My hair falls into my face, and I'm half tempted to leave it there, to let it shield my face from Alice's gaze, but I don't. If anyone is going to believe me here, it's going to be her. "Anyway, obviously, I didn't leave. So today, I saw him again, and he cornered me after class. I let him think I was going to give him a blow job, and then I busted his balls together, and I mean *literally* busted them together."

"Oh, my god," Alice tries not to laugh, but she can't do much to hide the grin on her face. "What's his name? Maybe I know him."

"Parker Rothschild." As soon as the name falls off my lips, Alice's smile completely vanishes.

"Willow," Alice grumbles and then presses her hand to her forehead as if she has a headache or something. "If your families hate each other, then why get involved with him?" Saliva turns to cement in my mouth, and Alice continues talking, "There is a reason the campus police did nothing and why no one will help you, not even if you beg and plead for it."

I chew on the inside of my cheek until I taste blood, "What do you mean? He can just hurt me, and no one will care? I don't understand how that's possible." Have we suddenly gone back in time?

Alice's hands fall from her face, and when our eyes meet, I see the fear and nervousness there. "He can do whatever he wants. His dad funds half the school programs and helped buy a new science lab last year. There was even a scandal a year or two ago where the assistant principal stole a bunch of money. He bailed them out, and so essentially the school, and all of the people who work here are indebted to him." *Christ.* My lungs start to deflate like balloons. There is no escaping him, and I've just gone and poked the bear. I've literally started a war with the one person I wanted to avoid most.

"They own this school and all the people who work here. If Parker tells someone to do something, they do it." Alice frowns, and doubt like I've never felt before starts to take root.

What have I done?

"What do I do?" I question nervously.

Alice shrugs, and her eyes move to the floor, "Lay low, and stay out of his way? I don't really know. But what I do know is that I don't want to get involved in this. I'm your friend, Willow, but Parker is bad news, and being noticed by him is even worse."

I'm not just shocked. I'm flabbergasted. It's like someone has pulled the rug right out from underneath me. Like they're standing on the sidelines watching as I slip, waiting for the moment when I fall, so they can attack.

This is wrong, so wrong, and all over again, I feel trapped, just like I did with the incident with my sister. Boiling with anger, I get up from the bed and move away from Alice. She's supposed to be my friend, but it feels like she's anything but that right now. As if she can feel my anger, she pipes up.

"Look, I'm sorry, but I don't want anything to do with Parker; he's dangerous, and I've heard horror stories about girls that get involved with him and his friends."

She visibly shivers, and I want to tell her she has no idea, but I bite my tongue.

"I just don't understand how they can get away with hurting people. How teachers can turn a blind eye to that behavior?" And I don't. I truly don't understand it.

"I don't know either, but I don't want you to get hurt because of Parker and his friends. Maybe he'll forget about what happened today?"

"Doubtful..." I mutter.

"What if you apologize to him?"

"*Me*, apologize to *him*?" What is this? Opposite day? She has to be insane if she thinks I'm going to apologize when I'm the victim in this.

"I get it, Willow. I know it's not right. In a perfect world, he would be the one apologizing to you, but we both know that this is not the way it works. Not anywhere, and especially not here at Blackthorn. Here, money and power are everything, and that's exactly what Parker and his family have, so while I'm sorry and you might hate it, I think tucking in your tail and apologizing is your best option right now."

I can't fucking believe this. Like I'm actually shocked. There are a thousand things I want to say, but none of the words come. The worst part of all is that there isn't one person in this entire place that would take my side over his. Alice might, but she wouldn't vocalize it. She wouldn't actually stick up for me.

"I know you don't want to do it, but you should. Just bite the bullet, apologize, grovel a little, and he'll probably leave you alone."

I blink, staring boulders through her face. She has to be high, or on some sort of drug.

"You can't be serious?"

She nods, "I am. If you want to remove the target from your back, then you'll have to apologize. It's that or walk around campus worrying that he'll come for you at any turn…"

My teeth grind together so hard my jaw starts to ache. Alice doesn't know anything; she doesn't understand that there is no stopping what I've done. Apologizing won't fix this. This kind of hate, this kind of anger, it's something that's been building for years.

I've essentially dug my own grave by provoking him. Now it's all about surviving, getting to the next day without being noticed. Flopping back on my bed, I stare up at the ceiling.

What the hell am I going to do?

THREE DAYS HAVE PASSED since I decided to sign my own death certificate. Like a crazed person, I watch over my shoulder waiting for him to strike, but so far, nothing's happened.

By the afternoon, I'm dreading every class I go to because I know; eventually, he's going to be in one of them. I can't outrun him forever. That point is proven when I walk into Biochemistry and see Parker sitting at one of the tables. A shiver runs through me from the top of my head all the way down to my toes.

I'm surprised to see another familiar face sitting right next to him. It's the guy from brunch, *Warren*. I stop mid-step and stare at them as they laugh at something together. Their laughter is like acid raining down on me. I doubt him talking to me that day was a coincidence.

I can tell the moment that Parker notices I've entered the room because it seems to grow quieter, the air becoming heavier. He looks up at me then, not an ounce of emotion showing on his beautiful, cruel face. He expected me to be here. Somehow, he knew I was going to be in this class. I just know it.

With my throat in my stomach, I make my way to a nearby open seat. I feel vulnerable with my back to him, but there isn't anything I can do about it. Steeling my spine, I tell myself I can do this. He's one person, in a sea of thousands. He isn't the first person to bully me, and he won't be the last. I've considered what Alice and I talked about. Apologizing, groveling, as badly as I don't want to, and I really don't want to, it might be my only option.

The hair at the back of my neck stands on end, and even though there are people talking around me, all I can hear and feel is him. My body is hyper-aware of his presence like an invisible rope is tethering us to each other. Barely being able to pay any attention to the professor, I almost miss what he is saying.

"For the first half of the semester, we are going to be working in groups. Divide the work evenly. Grades will be given to groups, not individuals," Dr. Dawson goes on, explaining how to set up and divide work within the group. I look around and watch as people are already moving and building groups of three or four people.

Shit. I must've been lost in thought for a lot longer than I thought.

Getting up, I walk over to the closest table. It's a group of three girls, and they're chatting quietly about how the class is a real pain in the ass.

"Hi, room for one more in your group?" I ask, in the friendliest way I can muster.

"Yes, but not for you," one of the girls mumbles without even looking up at me. Blinking slowly, I take a step back toward my table. *What the hell?*

Another one of the girls glances up at me, a condescending sneer on her red painted lips, "Run along, we don't want you here." She waves me on like I'm some forsaken being, and already I can feel the steam building in my head.

I don't know who I want to hit more right now, this chick or Parker. They might be rude, but I know for sure that Parker is the one putting them up to this. Why else would they act that way? Shaking my head, I move on to the next already formed group. I don't even get the chance to ask a question before they all start to shake their heads, giving me an answer without even knowing what I want. By the time I reach the third group, I'm gritting my teeth, my palms clenched into tight fists.

They do a mixture of what both groups had done before, shaking their heads and shoving rude comments my way. *Of fucking course.* There's only one group left… and that's Parker's group. Turning on my heels, I walk over to him, coming to a halt right in front of his table. I'm so close, I can smell his aftershave, clean and spicy. The scent goes straight to my head for a moment and my mouth waters. I want to kick myself for enjoying the smell, for even thinking of him in any way other than a monster. Swallowing down the thought, I hold on to the anger instead.

"I'm guessing you have something to do with this?" I question through my teeth.

Carrying on with his conversation with Warren, Parker completely ignores me. Asshole.

"Did you want me to be part of *your* group, is that it?" I ask, growing more irritated with him by the second.

He finally stops talking to Warren, but only long enough to turn toward me and say, "No, I don't want you here, and neither does anyone else, I thought that much was obvious?" His dark brow lifts in question, and my mouth pops open to respond, but before I can get a word out, he's talking again. "Shut your mouth. I wouldn't want you to dig yourself a deeper hole, so move along... no one wants you here, least of all me."

He dismisses me like I'm some kind of servant and turns back to Warren, who I see out of the corner of my eye is grinning from ear to ear. My cheeks heat with embarrassment. He's a god here, and I'm a mere mortal. I've basically been exiled.

Fuming, I stomp back to my seat and flop down in it. Crossing my arms over my chest, I stare straight ahead. Like a pouting child, I ignore the laughing and giggling within the room that is no doubt at my expense. I hate him. I hate him so much. Not just because of who he is, or our pasts. No, I literally hate him. I want to hurt him the same way he's hurting me.

After a few minutes, Dr. Dawson looks up from his computer, and I already know what's going to happen next. His eyes scan the room and of course, come to land on me immediately.

"You need to find a group," he orders, his voice low, leaving no room for argument.

"I work best on my own," I snap back.

"Too bad, this class requires a group assignment. Find a group or fail the class." He shrugs.

"I guess I'll be failing then," I grit out through clenched teeth while gathering my stuff. What did Parker expect? That I would get on my knees and beg him? *Fat chance.* Just as I get done shoving my things into my bag, I hear Parker's thick chuckle behind me. It's heavy and leaves a warmth in its wake.

"Don't be so dramatic. You can be in our group," Parker offers, and I'm half tempted to turn around and toss my textbook in his face.

"There you go," Dr. Dawson claps his hands together, "go sit with your group and start going over your assignment. You've wasted enough time."

Fucking asshole. Grabbing my stuff, I turn around and walk over to Parker's table. I'd rather eat glass than deal with him right now, but if I fail this class, I can't imagine what my father will do to my sister.

It's one class. One class, Willow. Shoving into a seat one over, so I'm not too close to Parker, I open the textbook and read over the assignment on enzymes- function, kinetics, and mechanism. The words alone give me a headache.

"I'll do part one, Warren part two, and you can do the rest," Parker says all matter of fact. This just keeps getting better and better. I open my mouth to protest being given sixty percent of the work when the classroom door flies open, interrupting me.

Looking up, I find yet another familiar face entering the room. *Nate.* Just when I thought my mood couldn't sour any further, he walks in. Nerves root me in place, and I feel like I might throw up.

Nate and Parker have been friends forever, but their friendship pales in comparison to the one he has with Parker's brother, Brett. An involuntary shiver ripples through me at the thoughts assaulting me. I never liked Nate. There was a time—two years ago, to be exact—when I actually liked Parker and Brett, but after everything that happened... *Yeah, no. Not going there.* Even as I stare down at the textbook, I can feel Nate's dark gaze roaming over me. He's always given me the creeps. I guess the Rothschild brothers were better at hiding their fuck up.

Not surprisingly, Nate comes and sits with us, and the teacher doesn't even make a comment about his tardiness.

"Willow, fancy seeing you here," he greets, showing only a little bit of shock as he takes the chair next to me. Everything about him makes me anxious.

Without even knowing what he's up to, I want to distance myself from him. Sitting down, he scoots even closer, so close that his thigh is touching mine. Instinctively, I slide away from him, and all the way to the corner of the table. The only reason I don't scoot around the corner is the fact that Parker is sitting on that side. No matter the way I go, I'm screwed, so I'll pick the least venomous of snakes.

"Hi, Nate," I mumble and flip open my textbook. He drapes his thick arm over the back of my chair, and it takes everything in me not to recoil. I don't know what it is about him, but I just can't stand him. Something about his presence leaves me feeling sick. When I glance up from my book, I find Parker staring at me, a prying look in his eyes. He doesn't seem to care about Nate sitting next to me, but he doesn't seem to like it either.

Pushing all the thoughts that circle these guys away, I try to concentrate on the assignment, but Nate's closeness has me on edge, even more so than Parker and Warren combined.

When the class is finally over, I can't stuff my book into my bag quick enough. Shoving it inside, I move to shove off my chair, but I'm stopped by Nate, who rests his hand on my arm. His touch burns through my skin, and while it isn't hurtful, I know it can be, will be. Nate doesn't just threaten. He follows through.

"Where are you going in such a rush, sweet cheeks."

"To another class," I lie, stopping my lip from wobbling, "let go of me, unlike you, I don't want to be late."

"You don't have another class today," Parker pipes up with a growl, "I got your class schedule, so I know you are lying. Of course, that's nothing new to you, right? Lying is your thing, after all." Nevermind the fact that he called me a liar for the hundredth time, he's now taken things to a whole new level.

"Why the hell do you have my class schedule?"

"I don't like surprises," he shrugs, and the dark hue of his eyes seems to lighten. "Why don't we stay here and go over the assignment again. Nate doesn't know which section he needs to do." I shake my head in response. *I'm not stupid.* I wouldn't stay here alone with Parker, let alone the three of them. It's not going to happen.

All is well until I try to get up again, and Nate tightens his grip.

"You're hurting me," I grit out as his meaty fingers dig into my skin with a bite.

"Behave, and I won't hurt you," he tells me in a low voice so only we can hear.

I look around the mostly cleared out room. Two other students and the professor are the only people left, and even they are heading for the door now. For a moment, I actually think about screaming or at least asking Dr. Dawson for help, but then again, what is he going to do? Not even the police were willing to help me. No one is brave enough to stand up to the Rothschilds.

I do my best to swallow down my fear because the last thing I want them to know is that I'm truly terrified because then, like sharks in blood infested waters, they'll attack.

The professor doesn't even look back as he pulls the door

closed behind him, leaving me alone with Parker, Warren, and Nate.

Alone in this room, I feel like a helpless lamb that's been led into the lion's den.

Question is; which lion from their pack will strike first?

6

PARKER

Strong. Fragile. Beautiful. Willow's fear is intoxicating, especially as she does her best to hide it. The air is thick between us, tensions so high, I'm sure everybody in class could feel it.

We're alone in the room now. Only Willow, Warren, Nate, and I left. Thoughts of what we could do to her run wild in my mind. Every one of them pumping blood straight to my dick. I could strip her bare, taunt her, taste her, mark her beautiful skin...

Nate licks his lips, and I catch his eyes roaming down Willow's body. I'll bet he's thinking of a million different things he can do to her. *Not today. Not ever.* He reaches out for her, and she jerks away, wincing when his fingers sink deeper into her snowy flesh. My jaw aches as my molars grind together.

"Don't bruise her skin," I order, "I'm the only one who gets to mark her."

"What do you want?" Willow growls at me, baring her teeth like she is trying to intimidate me. She doesn't seem to notice that I've just taken a step to protect her and instead turns her anger on me.

What do I want? I tap at my chin with my finger, acting as if I'm thinking. I already know what I want. I've thought about it often over the last three days. I want to hurt her. Make her pay, but I also want her body. I want to feel her come apart under my touch. I want her to scream my name with both pain and pleasure. Maybe I can combine those two?

"I told you what I wanted. I told you to leave, but you refused, so now we play my game, my way, and by my rules." I lean into her tiny little body, breathing in her intoxicating scent. Her beautiful eyes refuse to meet mine. What a shame.

"I warned you, Willow, and now I'm going to teach you a lesson, teach you that I'm in charge here. That I'm in charge of everything, everyone... including *you*."

I watch her shudder, and like the sick fuck I am, it makes me smirk.

Yes, Willow, be afraid... be very afraid.

"Nate, wait at the door and make sure no one gets in here."

"Why can't Warren do it?" He whines.

"'Cause I'm telling *you* to do it," I snap. I also don't like the way he looks at her like she's some piece of meat. She is mine. To hurt, to mark. Without looking over at Warren, I know he has a shit-eating grin on his face. I'll deal with him later, right now, I need to put on my best mask, and make sure Willow knows that I mean business.

At my word, Nate releases her with a shove and waltzes to the door, clearly irritated by my request. *Too fucking bad.*

"Get up," I tell Willow as I get up from my own seat.

"No," she growls, shaking her head. Her strength is arousing, but so is the thought of breaking her, of feeling her throbbing pulse beneath my hands.

"Get up, or I'll make you." I bark. At my threat, she gets up while staring daggers through me, and I'm sure if she could strike me dead with one single look, I'd be dead by now.

Warren gets up as well, and walks around the table, stopping at Willow's other side.

"Strip," I order, just to see if she would. I won't actually let her do it, not in front of my friends, but I want to see her reaction.

"What?!" Her eyes round with shock, her sexy little mouth popping open, and I wonder what she thinks we are going to do. Beat her up?

"You heard me. Strip, and do it slowly. I think you owe me a little show."

Fists clenched at her side, she curls her pink lip, "I owe you nothing!"

"Strip," I repeat, my voice harder.

"Fuck you!" She spits and I smirk. I figured she wouldn't do it, but it's fun to see her all worked up.

"Warren, hold her." My words have barely left my lips when Warren is behind her, grabbing hold of her wrists. She struggles, but he overpowers her easily, pulling her arms behind her back. I step directly in front of her, grabbing onto her shoulders to immobilize her further.

"You really shouldn't have done what you did." Her eyes go wide with fear, but I have to give her props, she doesn't scream or cry like I expected her to. All she does is stare at me, a sneer on her lips and fire in her eyes that tells me she's a little too proud to beg for my forgiveness right now.

With her chin held high, she opens her mouth to speak again. "Fuck you. You're nothing but a sicko who gets off on hurting people."

I should probably be offended by her accusation, but instead, I smirk, because the truth is, she isn't wrong. I do get off on hurting people. People who hurt my family, people like her...

With her arms pinned behind her back, I make use of the

freedom and reach for the button of her skinny jeans. If my cock weren't already harder than steel, it would be now.

Undoing the button and zipper, I watch with calculated eyes as her whole body stiffens, her chest rising and falling rapidly, drawing my attention to her perky breasts that remain hidden underneath her sweater.

I would love to strip her bare right now, right here on the table, next to the beakers and burners in the center. To open her legs and see her pretty pussy, to find out if she's as innocent as she looks. The only thing stopping me is my two douchebag friends being here. I don't like them seeing too much of her, I don't want to share what's mine.

So instead, I do the next best thing.

With her pants undone, I slowly move my fingers just inside her waistband, listening at the uptick of her breath. Her face is a mask that I can't penetrate, at least not yet. The soft fabric of her silky panties connects with the pads of my fingers, and I bite back a groan. I had always envisioned her to be a silk and lace kind of girl. I smirk, seeing her hardened nipples poking through the fabric of her sweater.

My mouth waters and I'm too tempted not to give in to the need to touch that hard little peak. With my thumb and forefinger, I pluck at the nub rolling it between two fingers. I fight the enticing need to shove her sweater up and take it into my mouth, to suck on it, to leave bright red marks on the milky white skin.

A low whimper meets my ears, as I pinch her nipple, twisting just enough to give her a bite of pain. Part of me wants to hurt her, to make her bleed, while the other part of me wants to touch her tenderly and watch her fall apart beneath my fingers.

No. Grappling for control, I release her nipple and ignore her whimpering. I make my way underneath her panties with my other hand. She's not objecting, not begging me to stop, which means she's either not scared enough yet, or she wants this just as badly as I do. And I guess I'm going to find out. My fingers find purchase on her skin a moment later. It's smooth and velvety, softer than her panties even.

Very slowly, I slide my hand lower, reveling in how she feels beneath my touch, bare and smooth. She smells even more delicious and looks even more tempting this close up. The last time we were this close darkness surrounded us, taking away my chance to see her, but this time, I can see her, burning like a ball of fire in the sky.

When I reach the top of her folds, I groan. I was prepared for her to scream, to cry, and beg me to stop, but nothing could have prepared me for the wetness I find when I slide my fingers through them.

Leaning into her, I pin her trembling body between Warren and me. Brushing my nose against her throat, I place an open-mouthed kiss against the tender skin, feeling her heartbeat thrum like a pair of bird wings against my lips.

"You're fucking wet," I confirm, slightly shocked while murmuring against her neck, just as I graze her swollen clit. With my own heart beating out of my chest, I move my fingers through her wetness, paying special attention to her tiny little nub, wishing my mouth was where my fingers are right now. I bet she'd taste absolutely delicious. Like chocolate and sin. Like a fucking liar...

Looking at her face, I find her eyes, as well as her lips, are squeezed shut, her face turned away from me. She's trying to ignore me, ignore this, but not even she can muffle the moan of pleasure enough to hide it. It vibrates through her whole body and into mine, her desire slamming into me like a hurricane barreling against the coastline.

Fuck. My jaw clenches, and suddenly I realize I want to feel her fall apart on my hand. The plan was to scare her, but now I want more, need more, and she's the perfect victim.

She took from me, so I suppose it's okay for me to take from her.

Taking her clit between my index and middle finger, I alternate between pinching it and rubbing small circles against it at the same time, drawing another groan out of her. Her cheeks turn a soft pink, and she struggles against Warren, almost as if she's trying to fight the mounting pleasure, but no matter how much she tries to hide it, she can't hide the fact that her body wants me. It wants my touch.

Nipping at her ear, I whisper, "I warned you, and you should have listened." I pinch her clit, smirking as she bites down on her bottom lip to stifle the pleasure she's feeling. "I own this place, and everybody in it, including you. You do what I say when I say it. If I want you naked and, on your knees, then you better be naked and on your fucking knees." I bite her ear again, and she shivers, from fear or pleasure, I don't know, but if I'm betting, I'm going to say pleasure.

"I own you now, and that means I own your body too, and I bet you can guess what that means?" I give her a moment to answer, and when she doesn't, I chuckle, blowing hot breath against her skin. "Since you don't want to answer, I'll be nice and tell you. It means I'm going to do with you whatever I want, whenever I want, do you understand?" My words seem to only arouse her more because as soon as they pass my lips, I feel a gush of moisture against my fingers. She's like a waterfall, gushing with arousal, and I'm a man who hasn't had a drink of water in years.

"You can't do this," her lips tremble, and while it sounds like she's afraid, she's not telling me to stop, and that's good enough for me. I want this, need this. I've waited three long days to feel her beneath me. It's time to watch the fragile beauty fall apart at my touch. If she remembers anything, it'll be how she wanted this as badly as I did.

"I can, and I'm going to." Confidence oozes from every pore

in my body as I move my fingers lower, till I'm grazing her entrance.

"Would you fuck her already, we don't have all day," Nate calls from the door and like a dog with a bone, I turn and pierce him with a look that would normally be reserved for my enemies. Something he's going to find himself if he doesn't knock it the fuck off.

Unphased by the look, the asshole rolls his eyes at me, and I make a mental note to slug him in the face later. Directing my attention back to Willow, I grip her by the chin with my other hand, my hardened touch causing her big green eyes to flutter open.

Using my middle finger, I press it against her drenched cunt, exhaling as it slips inside her with ease. Her lips part, a soft sigh exhaling from them. She closes her eyes again, but I like seeing her. In her eyes, I can see how vulnerable she is, how much she wants this, and I need that. I need to be able to see that this is a punishment and nothing more.

"Open your eyes," I command. "I want you to look at me while you come all over my finger." I half expect her to close her eyes out of spite, just because she wants to defy me wherever she can. Instead, she surprises me by keeping them open, staring up at me without even blinking it seems. All her fight and defiance are diminishing by the second, leaving a good amount of lust behind.

Breathing heavily now, her perfectly straight white teeth sink into her pouty bottom lip, probably in an attempt to keep herself from moaning. I slide my finger in as deep as I can, all while keeping the rough pad of my thumb on her clit, drawing small circles against it.

Cum beads the tip of my cock, and like a teenage boy, I wonder if Willow has the power to make me come in my jeans. Of course, she does, she's the one temptation I can't give in to, the one thing my body craves.

Each second that passes makes her breathing grow rougher, her head twists from side to side as she fights against my touch, against each thrust of my finger into her tight little hole.

"Fall apart for me. I want to feel you gush all over my hand. I want to see what your face looks like when you realize what I can do to you... that I do own you."

She shakes her head furiously, a silky strand of her black hair flies into her face blocking half of it from view, but I don't have to see her eyes to know what she's feeling. Moving my finger faster, I put more pressure against her clit. I can see she is close, feel it, smell it even, her arousal cloaks the air making it hard for me to breathe.

Releasing her chin, I move my hand back to her perky breast, finding her nipple, I squeeze it through her sweater and bra. At the onslaught of sensations her head falls back against Warren's chest, I'd almost forgot he was here at all. The muscles in my arm strain, my entire body begging for me to just strip her bare and fuck her out of my mind.

Her green eyes glaze over, and that pretty fucking mouth forms a perfect *O* moments before she shatters, coming apart right down the middle. Her pussy clenches around my finger, so tight and warm, I almost come in my pants, thinking about how my cock would feel inside of her right now.

"Fuck.... So tight and warm." I grit out, continuing to rub her swollen nub until it stops pulsing, and I know her orgasm has rippled through her completely. Regretfully, I pull my hand out of her pants. Even if I want to spend all day there, I can't. I can't let her know how weak I am for her; how much I crave her. She's like a drug, addicting, pulse-pounding.

Like an addict seeking out his next fix, I bring my finger to my mouth, the same one that was just inside her. Sucking the digit into my mouth, I let her tangy juices explode against my tongue. She watches me through hooded eyes, her breathing still uneven but not as erratic as it was a few minutes ago. Her cheeks are a bright red now, her entire body still trembling. She leans back against Warren, and I bet if it weren't for him holding her, she'd be on the ground.

"Next time, it will be your turn," I tell her before taking a step back. I want to take her into my arms, take her with me back to my house, but I can't. Won't. She's nothing but trouble, nothing but a fucking liar, and I can't forget that, no matter how tempting she is, no matter how sexy she looks when she falls apart.

"Let's go, Warren."

With her pants still undone, Warren releases her with a shove toward the table. Her hands fly out, and she grabs onto the edge to steady herself. I curl my hands into fists to stop myself from reaching out to her, and instead, take another step back. My chest heaves, and it feels like I can't breathe. I may not have come, but it still feels like she took a piece of me with her when she fell off that ledge.

Forcing my hands to uncurl, I adjust my jeans against my strained cock and walk away without looking back. Warren is by my side when I reach the door. Brushing by Nate, I ram my shoulder into his. He doesn't say anything thankfully and simply shakes his head, falling into step as I walk out and into the hallway.

With every step I take, I try my best to get the image of her face as she came out of my brain, but I don't know why I try. I already know it'll forever be branded in my mind.

7

WILLOW

I can't believe what just happened. I'm in the science lab on my own now. My pants are still undone, my panties are soaked, and my pussy is throbbing from the intense release I just experienced. As I'm coming down from the endorphin rush, dread starts to set in my bones.

Parker just made me come…but that's not the worst part. He did it in front of his friends. He did it to prove a point, that he owns this place, that he owns me, my body, my feelings they're all his. I feel humiliated, dirty, and used.

When my breathing has evened out, and my heartbeat has returned to a somewhat normal rhythm, I stand up a little straighter. My knees are still shaking, and my stance is unsure as I button and zip up my pants.

Part of me wants to remain in this classroom, hiding from the world, while the other wants to run out, to run away and never come back here. What the hell am I going to do? What the hell was I thinking provoking him like that? My hands tremble as I stare at them.

"Next time it will be your turn…" his words run on a loop through my head. What did he mean? That I'll jerk him off?

Jesus, what is wrong with him, but more importantly, what's wrong with me? How could I have been so aroused by this? Why was I so wet? Why am I still thinking about what happened? And if it's going to happen again. *No, no... this is all wrong.*

The more the fog of arousal is lifted from my mind, the clearer my thoughts become. This is so fucked up. Parker is fucked up, and I need to get away from him. He's just proven that he has no boundaries. He thinks he can do whatever he wants, and in a way, I guess he can, but that doesn't mean I have to let him do anything to me again.

Taking my phone out of my bag, I unlock the sleek device with trembling hands. I don't want to do this, but I feel cornered, trapped. Looking through my contact list, I scroll to the last person I want to call, but the only one who can actually help me in my current situation. I push the green call button and hold the phone to my ear.

After a few rings, my father finally picks up.

"Willow," his stern voice comes through the line, and if I wasn't feeling like crap before, I am now, knowing that I have to do this. "How is everything going at Blackthorn?"

"Not good, Dad," I admit. "Not good at all." I sigh into the empty room, knowing that nothing good is going to come of this phone call.

"What did you do, Willow?" Of course, he blames me. He has no idea what I'm calling about, but his first thought is that I did something wrong. It's times like these that I wish my mother were still alive. If she were here, nothing would've ever happened to Ashton... I wouldn't be here now, a pawn in my father's sick chess game.

"I didn't do anything unless you count being alive and being here, wrong, which apparently Parker does." I'm trying really hard not to sound like a whiny little brat, but it's harder than you'd expect. I hate being here already, and I hate that he's here even more. "Dad, I can't do this. I can't be here. He hates me, he threatens me constantly, and he—"

"Willow," my father cuts me off. "Stop being so dramatic and do what I told you to do. If Parker is there and noticing you, then that's exactly what we want."

No, it's what you want.

"It's wrong, he wants me to sleep with him. I—"

"What's the issue then? If he wants you, then use that to your advantage. Sleep with him, wrap him around your finger. Do whatever it takes to get into his good graces."

What?

I hold the phone away for a moment, looking at the screen, hoping the phone might be broken or something. That would make more sense than him saying what he just said.

"You're kidding, right?" I bring the phone back to my ear. "You don't actually expect me to sleep with him... I mean, you can't really, right?" I feel like I'm in some horror movie that keeps playing on repeat, every time the killer kills me, I come back, reliving the same events over and over again.

"God, you are so dramatic. Don't act like you are some kind of saint who's saving herself for marriage. Spread your legs if you have to. You're a woman, that's what's going to get you places. It's how the world works, Willow, so don't blame me. I didn't make the rules. Just remember, sex is only what you make of it."

"No... I won't... that's... do you even hear yourself right now?" My stomach twists so violently I have to hold onto the side of the table.

Frustration burns through the phone line. "Look, Willow. I don't care if you sleep with him or not as long as you get into his circle of friends. Just make it easy on yourself and get it done soon. Your sister has cost me enough time and trouble, don't make the same mistakes she did. Just do what you're told."

Just be my puppet... that's all I hear.

"I'm not staying here. You can't expect me to, not with how insane he is. You don't understand. He's going to hurt me, he's already tried—"

My father chuckles into the phone, "Parker is a college kid, a fly, what's he going to do?" The better question would be, what isn't he going to do?

"You're perfectly safe there, and you'll remain there, that is unless you want your sister to be homeless?" The threat hangs in the air between us.

"So, we're back to threats, great, you're no better than Parker." I grip the phone hard enough to break it. I'm so tired of this. I dealt with it all last year, and this year I thought it would be better, different. But it's not, it's all just the same. Same shit, different day.

"Goodbye, Willow," he hangs up the phone without another word. *He just hangs up!* I'm not even sure what to say at this point.

Even more shocked than before this phone call, I stand in the center of the empty science lab. Tears prick at my eyes, and before I know it, they're falling, leaving streaks down my cheeks. I guess the only good thing about today is that I didn't cry in front of Parker and his friends.

I wanted to cry. I wanted to beg and plead, to tell him to stop, but I didn't. I knew better. It wouldn't have helped me any. What he did today, it was a warning, it could've been much worse, and it will be if I don't stay out of his way.

Peering down at my black phone screen, I know what I have to do.

∼

A FEW DAYS have passed since our run-in, and I'm about to head to English literature, one out of two classes I've been dreading going back to. I've managed to avoid Parker, at all costs, mainly by hiding out in my room, but I know I can't hide today, much less forever.

I've spent the last few nights thinking about what Alice and I had talked about, and as much as I hate to say it, I think apologizing is my best shot at being forgotten right now.

Maybe it will make things better. Perhaps if I explain that my father won't let me leave, that I overstepped, which I didn't, he'll understand. *Yeah, right.* That's wishful thinking.

It won't matter to Parker. He won't care, just like his brother didn't care that night. Shaking my head, I try not to think about my sister or even my father. No one can save me, protect me. There is just me.

Arriving early to class, I walk to the back of the room and take the same seat as last time. Parker isn't here yet, and thankfully so. I suck in a tiny breath of relief, thinking over what exactly I'm going to say to him. I've barely got my books out of my bag when Parker comes strolling down the aisle.

Half of the chairs are still empty, but of course, he chooses to take the one right next to me. *Because why not choose one of the twenty other empty seats?*

"Did you keep a seat for me?" he asks, a smug look on his arrogant, beautiful face. I want to come back with a snarky remark. Something like: you can shove that seat up your ass, but I swallow the insult down instead.

"Yes, actually... I wanted to talk to you."

He raises his eyebrows, looking thoroughly intrigued. "Yeah, is that so?"

"I wanted to apologize... ah for, kneeing you... you know in the..." I stumble over the words, and my stupid cheeks flame as if the sun is beating on them.

"Balls?" He finishes for me.

"Yes, for that." *Even though you deserved it,* I add in my head.

For a long moment, he just looks at me, studying me like I'm a math problem to be solved.

"Your words mean nothing to me," he blinks slowly, "however, you can come back to my place after class and *show* me how sorry you are."

"I..." I should have known he would say something like this, I'm still a little shocked. I take my bottom lip between my teeth. I know better, every single cell in my body is going off, blinking with a bright red sign telling me what a bad idea that would be. But if it's my only option, I can take this stupid mark off my back...

"Worried? Afraid?" He feeds right into my fear like he has a direct line to it.

Do I admit that I'm afraid, or do I just let him think whatever he wants? After what he did to me the other day, I doubt he cares about me being scared of him, or his friends, then again, he seems to be a little more composed now, less angry.

"If I do this, come to your house and do whatever... will you leave me alone afterward?"

Amusement flickers in his chocolate-brown depths, and I don't know why I'm trying to make a deal with the devil. "No, Willow. I won't ever leave you *alone*. Not as long as you are here at this school. I don't care how many times you apologize, nothing is going to erase what you did. You destroyed my brother's life with your lie. You destroyed mine."

"I didn't lie—" The words get cut off when Parker slams his fist on the table, making me, and the people sitting in front of us jump. The professor, who has already entered the classroom, glances over to us but doesn't say a word. Reminding me once again that no one is going to stand up to Parker.

I have the urge to get up and run out of the class, to leave Parker behind, and find someone to talk to. Trouble is, I have no one. Even Alice has been distancing herself from me.

Ever since I told her about what happened, she's been avoiding me, going as far as staying somewhere else overnight instead of in our shared dorm room. I'm alone in this, completely alone. I never should've come here. Never.

"That's the problem with you, Bradford girls. All you do is lie and manipulate and..." Parker is reaching his boiling point, lips curled, and the edges of his face hardened, making him appear more like a brooding statue. He's a bomb, and I'm watching, waiting for him to detonate.

"Look, I'm sorry, Parker... I didn't..."

Anger pours out of him, and I shiver at the image before me as he leans in, his face mere inches from my own. I can smell the mint on his breath, feel his anger as it charges the air.

"Shut up. I don't want to hear you speak, or even breathe. As long as you remain here, you will be mine. I thought I made that clear the other day, or do I need to remind you again?"

I shake my head without even thinking. Being humiliated by him once was enough, but to go through it again. No, I won't survive another incident like that. I'm already tired of being his punching bag. His nostrils flare, and his gaze hardens further. My own aggravation mixes with fear, and I realize then that I'm doing exactly what he told me to. Sinking further in my seat, I open my books up and face the front of the room, pretending like he's not there at all.

"Good girl, now maybe later I'll reward you. Or maybe I'll punish you. Just remember to be seen and not heard." And like a fucking dog who has just done a trick, he pats me on the head and settles into the seat beside me. I don't know how I do it, but somehow, I manage to bite my tongue. As class goes on, doubt starts to build in my gut. *When will I learn?* When will I realize that no matter what I say to him, no matter what proof I have against Brett, he will never believe me? In his eyes, Ashton and I are to blame and not his brother. Forget apologizing to him. I'm done. I'll just lay low from here on out.

I almost laugh at the thought. Like he's going to let that happen. No, Parker is out to terrorize me, to hurt me. The professor starts class, and the temperature in the room grows hotter and hotter. Sitting this close makes it impossible to ignore him. His spicy scent, every little twitch of his jaw, or bulge of his bicep. I notice it all. *Feel* it all. Deep down in my core.

He leans over as I try and focus on whatever it is the professor is saying. "Are you thinking about it?" He chuckles. "My fingers in your pussy? What it would feel like to have my cock there instead?"

No. Yes. "No. I'd rather nail my hand to the wall than sleep with you."

"I can make that happen too if you're into that kind of thing. Although, nailing your hand to anything seems a little extreme. I think we should start by tying you to the bed, then work ourselves up from there…"

"What the fuck is wrong with you?" I snap, my voice way louder than I intended it to be. My cheeks warm, my entire body feeling as if it's reached its boiling point.

Someone clears their throat, and when I look up, I realize it was the professor, who is still looking at me with an annoyed expression on his face. *I just can't catch a break.* What is this insanity? Does he really own this school and all the people in it? I guess so.

Whispers spread across the room, and when I look around, I realize everyone is looking at me. Some sneer, while others just stare in horror. I feel like I'm the freak at the carnival that everyone's come to see. Pressure builds behind my eyes, and I know if I don't calm down right now, I'm going to start crying.

Breathe, Willow, breathe.

You can do this. Think of your sister. Think of all she's been through. She won't get better if she doesn't have you. The thoughts help soothe the ache forming in my chest, and just as I'm becoming somewhat composed again, Parker leans in. "You still haven't learned your place." His voice is low and raspy as he continues whispering into my ear. "Let me remind you... since you've forgotten. It's on your knees, in front of me... naked, with my dick in your mouth. That's where you belong and where you will be right after this class. I'm done waiting. If I have to, I'll just take it from you..."

That's the last straw... I can't handle anymore. If it's not my father, it's Parker, and if it's not them, then it's Ashton. I'm slowly drowning, and the people around me see it, yet they keep putting rocks in my pockets, making me sink deeper and deeper.

"You know what I'm done with?" I reply, anger finally boiling over. "You! I'm done with you and your games." Furiously, I shut my books, the noise draws the attention of the rest of the room, but who cares, it doesn't matter. They were all laughing at me before. What's another show? Shoving out of my chair, I don't even bother to pack up my stuff. I just grab my bag and my phone and walk out of the room.

Fuck him, fuck this school, and fuck my dad.

8
PARKER

I sit on a bench outside, tapping my pencil against the bind of my English textbook. I'm supposed to be studying, but the sun is setting, I wish the light were my excuse, but honestly, I just can't stop thinking about her. About my next move.

I dial Alice's number knowing once she's gone from the situation, I'll have Willow all to myself. The phone rings twice before she picks up. "Hello," her apprehensive voice comes through the line.

"Alice, it's Parker again. Did you do what I asked you to do?"

"Yes, I moved out this morning, but I don't understand why you wanted me to do this." The worry in her voice would be a concern if I gave a fuck, but I don't.

"You don't have to understand, all you have to do is what I say, and you'll have nothing to worry about." Pressing the red end key, I hang up before she can say anything else.

I've only seen Willow from afar this week. For days she disappeared, but only after making a huge scene. Only after proving once again, that she didn't know her place in this kingdom. After she stormed out of English literature last week, she hasn't been back to class. Matter of fact, she hasn't left her dorm room much at all. I hate it. Not seeing her, not being able to torment her. I've kind of grown accustomed to doing and saying things that I know will get under her skin. It's become a drug. She's become a drug.

A sick feeling makes its way through my limbs at that knowledge. I know my stalking has reached new heights. My obsession growing like a cancer. My fingers itch to touch her, to peel back all her layers, to see if she's actually scared of me.

Maybe she's just as curious as I am about how good it would be if we came together. *No.* I snarl in anger, hating that I'm attracted to her at all. I think back on what my father said. *"Get your revenge, son. Do what you have to do to make her pay."*

I think about the first time Willow saw me here, and how I told her about attending. I smile at the memory. I knew then that I would do whatever it took to get my revenge. After the last few days, that's gotten harder for me. I can't get to her if she's hiding in her dorm.

But with Alice gone, there is nothing in my way. There is nothing stopping me from walking into that room and taking what I want. *What I deserve.* The thought has me on edge but in a good way. Like when you're on the crest of the big hill on the roller coaster, about to go over the top and down at a ninety-degree angle. I'm so excited, I almost can't wait until she's asleep. The energy rippling through me makes me want to get up and run laps around the room.

Looking into her window from the park across the dorm, I test my patience by waiting for her to turn off her lights. The seconds tick by, each one like a grain of sand falling from my hand and floating away in the breeze. I watch curiously as she sits on her bed, gazing down at something in her hands. Her face is downcast, and what appears to be a frown appears on her lips, then again at this distance, I can't really tell.

For some reason, I feel this tightness spread throughout my

chest, wondering if she feels as alone as I do? *Don't.* I tell myself. If I feel bad for her, then I might as well be agreeing with her, and the shitstorm she brought down on my family. No way in hell I'm doing that. She's the liar. My brother is innocent, paying for another man's crimes.

Another second ticks by. I tap my pencil a little faster, a little harder. My impatience mounts. Then, almost like she can tell I'm waiting, she turns the light off, and the room descends into darkness. My lips pull up into a smile that only I can feel the real joy of. I wait another ten minutes for good measure. I want her to be asleep. That's going to make this way more fun. The hunt is part of the thrill.

Walking into the dorms, I act as if I belong there, and I suppose I do. If it weren't for my father, this place would've gone under. So, in a way, this entire place belongs to my family and me. Which means no one can tell me to leave or to stop.

Getting antsier by the second, I take the steps two at a time until I reach her floor. Heading straight for her door, I fist the key card in my hand, the plastic biting into my palm. When I get to the door, I slowly slide the card through the slot, watching the small light turn green. *Bingo.* As quietly as I can, I push the door open. It doesn't even creak as I tiptoe into the room.

Stepping over the threshold, her unique scent washes over me, and stops me dead in my tracks. Damn her for being so tempting. As strange as it is, her smell calms my heated blood, and I automatically suck in a deep breath like it's a drug, and I'm an addict. A few more calming breaths, and I'm able to move again.

It's completely dark in the room, with only the dim light from the window to guide me, I can see the outlines of the furniture. Strange how our finest moments seem to happen in the dark. I close the door behind me, just as quietly as I opened it, my ears straining as I listen for her to make any noise. When

I hear nothing besides her even breathing, I smirk. She's asleep, sound asleep, just as I'd hoped. Silently, I walk toward her bed, the shadows of the room protect me, and I stop when I'm only a foot away. Even if she opened her eyes right now, she wouldn't see me.

Like the total creep I am, I stand there and watch her for a second, until my eyes have adjusted to the darkness, and I can see the contours of her perfect face better. My muscles ache, and a knot twists deep in my gut. My heart is pounding against my ribs so furiously, I'm surprised she hasn't woken from the noise.

Taking one final exhale, I get ready to strike. I count down in my head. Three. Two. One. Like a feral cat stalking its prey, I pounce on her. Positioning myself on top of her, I slap a hand over her mouth to muffle the screams that are soon to come.

Her whole body goes rigid for a second before she turns into a wild banshee, having realized that whatever is happening isn't just a nightmare, but reality. As I had suspected, she starts to wail, very much like a pig, but not much noise gets past my hand. Her struggle turns me on. Her fear, which I can already smell permeates the air, soaking into every pore.

She tries to buck me off by lifting her hips, and when that doesn't work, her hands land tiny insignificant hits against my chest. She struggles, trying to use her legs as a weapon against my crotch, but I easily overpower her with my weight alone.

She's a tiny little bug, and I'm a fucking giant.

Oh, how easy it would be to squish her right now.

"I hope you didn't think we were done?" I whisper against the supple skin on her neck. I want to bite her there, feel her pulse thunder against my lips. As soon as she hears my voice, she stops flailing, and her limbs fall to her sides. For half a second, I wonder why? Is she relieved that it's me, or is she simply petrified, realizing that it is me?

Was she expecting it to be someone else? The thought slams into me, a wave of carnal possession overtaking me. I want to roar from the rooftops that she is mine. Because she is, and she should know that by now. I've told and shown her plenty of times. This cat and mouse game we're playing, it can only end one way. With her beneath me, giving in to my every command.

"Did you think you could hide, and I wouldn't find you?" Part of me wants to shake her for being so stupid. "There is nowhere safe for you to hide, nowhere for you to go where I wouldn't find you." I lick my lips, and a strange desire pricks at my senses. It grips me by the throat. I've never wanted to experience something like this before.

I want to kiss her, just once, to see if she tastes as sweet as she looks. To see if she's as sour on the inside as I know her to be. It's a reckless thing to do. Stupid. Careless. If my father were here right now, he would be scolding me.

Never kiss them. Never show them emotion.

"I want to do something, but that means I have to remove my hand…" I whisper, my breath coming out in shallow pants now. "If you scream, I will hurt you… and right now that's the last thing I want to do, but that doesn't mean I won't. Test me, make one little peep, and I'll have you on your knees and my cock down your throat."

She nods her head profusely as if to tell me that she'll be quiet, and I smile against her skin. As I lift my hand off her mouth, I'm still expecting her to scream. If she were smart, she would. I'm feeling on edge tonight, walking the razor's edge between right and wrong, and I'm not sure how far I'll take things.

"What do you want?" Her groggy voice pierces through the heavy fog surrounding my head.

"*You*…I want to *feel* you. I want you to return the favor," I grind my stiffened cock into her. Willing her to feel the need that she brings out in me. I don't want to want her, but I do. I want her so badly it hurts. I crave her. I need her, but at the same time, I hate that it's this way. It used to be simpler, but then she went and opened her mouth... she went and lied.

Now my obsession is fueled by something darker, something far worse than need.

"No. I told you, I don't want you." Using her hands, she tries to shove against my chest, but my body doesn't even budge. Letting out a frustrated sigh, she continues, "Are you going to rape me? Like your brother raped my sister?" Her question catches me off guard, taking me out at the knees, and for one single second, I don't have a response for her.

"You are just like him...aren't you? You say he is innocent, but then you act like him. You're both fucked up."

Out of nothing more than pure reflex, my hand moves to her throat. Wrapping my fingers around the delicate column, I squeeze hard enough to cut off her words. She's lost her chance to talk. Now, if she wants a say, she'll have to fight for it.

"You're wrong... so fucking wrong. I'm nothing like my brother..." I almost laugh but instead tighten my grip further until she is gasping for air. The sound she makes goes straight to my cock, and I know it's wrong, so wrong, but it feels right. Her eyes bug out of her head, and her hands circle my wrists while her tiny nails dig into my skin, hard enough to draw blood.

Yes, hurt me, Willow.

Resting my cheek against hers, I loosen my grip, but only enough so she can suck in a labored breath. "See, I was always fucked up, the black sheep of the family. For as long as I can remember, there's always been a darkness around me, but Brett... he was the good one. He was the best thing in my life, my rock, my best friend, and you took him away from me."

"I didn't..." She gasps, and I raise my head, so I can look into her eyes again. Her green eyes brim with tears. Two big fat tears escape her eyes and slip down her cheeks, the cold droplets crash onto my hands. I'm not sure what it is that causes me to release her, the tears, or maybe the look in her eyes?

Yes, I want her to be afraid of me. Her fear is what makes my blood sing, but the way she's looking at me right now... like I might kill her? Yeah, I don't like that.

"You did. You ruined my family, you ruined him, and you ruined me, all with one single lie." I crawl backward off the bed, putting more distance between us because right now, I don't know which side of me will win out. The one that wants to own her, or the one that wants to destroy her.

Willow sits up, clutching the blanket to her chest like it could possibly save her from me. *What a joke.* Her black hair is in disarray, and her lips are swollen. Fuck, I didn't even get to kiss her. Not that she deserves a kiss... my first kiss. She deserves nothing, not to be here, and certainly not my attention.

"I didn't lie, Parker. I swear to you. He was there that night. I saw him leave..." Her words are like acid rain pouring down on me, eating away at my resolve. I don't want to hear her lies anymore. I don't want to hear anything but silence. *I. Need. Silence.* Without even thinking about my next move, I cross the space that separates us, thread my fingers in her hair and pull her to my face, crushing our lips together, sealing my hate for her with a punishing kiss. My movements are so quick that Willow has little time to react until the kiss is underway.

Gasping into my hungry mouth, she releases her hold on the blanket, so she can use both hands to push me away. She shoves against my chest, but her efforts are futile. I'm not letting go now, not now that I've kissed her. Now I'm going to taste, devour, own.

With a handful of her hair, I pull her head back, making her yelp in pain. Her mouth opens, and I take that opportunity to taste her. I slide my tongue past her lips and into her hot wet mouth. *Finally, she is mine.* She moans, and I feel the sound vibrating through me, all the way to my toes. I need her, want her.

Without thinking, I deepen the kiss, melting into her. Sliding onto the bed, my senses are overwhelmed by her, her smell, her taste, the feel of her skin against mine. I feel compelled to strip her bare and fuck her slowly and deeply. I want to feel her inside and out. Nothing could stop me.

One moment her small hands are pushing me away, and the next, they are wrapping around my neck, pulling me closer. This way, I can feel every shapely inch of her body through the flimsy camisole and sleep shorts she's wearing. Pebbled nipples press against my chest, and I bite back a groan. I want to suck them, bite them.

Willow moves beneath me, grinding herself against my body, bringing my attention elsewhere. With her slim arms wrapped around my neck, she pulls me closer, almost like she can't get enough of me. Like the air, and our clothing is still too much space.

Then something inside my brain snaps. I feel its effect all the way down my spine. *She wants this.* The reality of it is a motherfucker, and I sober up at the thought.

She wants this… she wants me.

Breaking the kiss, I untangle her arms from around my neck and push up from the bed, needing to put distance between us. We're both breathing heavily, and even in the dim light, I can see the shock written all over her face.

Does she think this is a game?

"What do you think you're doing?" I growl at her.

"Me?" Her voice goes high-pitched, and her brows shoot up her forehead. "You came into my room, got in my bed, tried to… god knows what…I didn't… You. You kissed me!" Her finger thrusts in my direction, and I'm half tempted to reach out and break it. I tamp the need down, but just barely…

"This whole time you pretended to hate me—"

"I do hate you!" She interrupts me.

"You didn't hate me a minute ago when you were clawing at my back to get closer." I hate this... this power she has. How weak I become when I think of her being mine. "This is not how it works. This is not for your pleasure. You don't get to make the rules. I do." I seethe, my jaw aching with the pressure of my clenched teeth.

Willow doesn't seem to be fazed by my newly found anger. In fact, she looks as if she's poised for a fight. "You might make the rules, and you might have all the power around here, but you can't tell me how to feel. You will never have that power over me. You will never control my mind."

And just like that, I'm back to wanting to wrap my hands around her throat. Instead, I curl them into fists, digging my nails into my palms. She's making me lose control. We're chaos riding a slippery slope into hell, and if we're not careful, we'll both get burnt to a crisp.

"Do you want me to hurt you, Willow? Do you want to see what happens when I lose control?" My voice drops, and something inside of me snaps.

Willow's gaze hardens and lifts in defiance. I can see the fire flickering in her eyes. She wants to push me. To see how far I'll go, and that only enrages me further, that she has this power over me, the power to make me lose control.

Ticking like a bomb, I try and rein in the anger. Breathing usually helps, but not today. Her scent surrounds me, suffocating me, reminding me further... unable to resist, I twist around and pull my fist back, slamming the thing into the wall. Willow's soft gasp tickles my ears, and I curl my lip with satisfaction.

Pain lances up my arm and my teeth rattle inside my head at the impact, but the euphoric waves that ripple through me, make me grin like a sick fuck. Pain, pleasure, it all feels the same. Turning, I pin Willow with an icy glare that I know penetrates that feeble heart of hers.

"Stay the fuck out of my way, or you'll regret it. Don't come to class. I don't want to see you…"

"Don't threaten me with a good time, Parker," her voice is provoking, and if I stay in this room another second, I might make good on all the things the little devil on my shoulder is whispering in my ear.

"Watch your back, Bradford," I smirk like a crazed person, knowing more is to come, so much more. I'll have her on her knees and her back, but first, I have to get my own thoughts and feelings under control. Willow might've won this round, but next time, I won't show mercy.

9

WILLOW

It's official, Parker is psychotic. I assumed that he was before, but now I know without a doubt that he truly is. I can still feel his fingers digging into my skin. His hot breath against my cheek. My heart hammers in my chest like a jackhammer. I'm just as fucked up because part of me wasn't scared, part of me liked it, liked him on top of me, pinning me to the bed. Taking from me what I wasn't sure I wanted to give. I shake my head. Maybe I'm even more fucked up than him. I try and focus on my homework, paging through the textbook, but all I can think about is what happened between us, and how it made me feel.

The sun hangs high in the afternoon sky, peeking in through the window, reminding me that I haven't eaten lunch.

Still, hiding out in my room for most of the day, I wonder how long I can keep this up. My dad is going to find out sooner rather than later that I'm skipping class and doing the complete opposite of what he's asked me. This is bad, so bad. I'm not sure what to do, how to fix this. Things with Parker aren't that easy, they're complicated, twisted.

My phone rings and I'm so used to the quiet now that I

actually jump at the noise. No one has called me since... my mood goes from bad to rotten. *My dad.*

Picking up the phone, my worst fear is confirmed, it's daddy dearest calling, probably asking for an update on the mission he sent me on. I push the green answer button—even though I want to send him to voicemail—and hold the phone to my ear.

"Hello," I greet him, trying to hide the disdain in my voice.

"Willow, we have a situation," my father explains. "I'm with Ashton, she is not doing well at this facility." Panic claws at me from the inside out. What does he mean? I haven't talked to her in a while, but last I heard she was doing okay.

"What... what do you mean? Is she okay? Can I talk to her?" My lips tremble as I speak.

"She is stable now." He sounds annoyed like she's inconveniencing him. Gritting my teeth, I try not to think the worst.

"Stable?" What does that mean? That she wasn't at one point? "What's going on? You can't just say something like that without explaining."

"She tried to hurt herself again," my father explains.

"Let me talk to her, please." I hear some rustling, and a moment later, I hear her.

"Willow," she calls my name, and I can feel her pain through the phone. She's broken, so damn broken, and all I want to do is fix her, but I don't know how. The kind of help she needs doesn't come cheap, and without my father, she'll be on the streets, worse off than she is now. The reality is that I can't just give up on her. I can't.

"Ashton, what happened, why did you hurt yourself?"

"I'm sorry, Willow, I'm just so... I can't be here any longer. I can't. I want to leave this place, but Dad says the other place is too expensive."

Other place? What is going on that makes her want to leave? When she first went to the facility, she loved it there. Now all of a sudden she's spiraling out of control, she doesn't like it? Something bad must have happened.

"I don't understand, I thought you loved it there."

"I did before Dad had me moved here. I want to go back to the rehab I used to be at." It takes everything in me to hold on to the phone instead of throwing it against the wall in anger. That bastard had her moved. I should have known he was too cheap to keep her in that nice of a place. I don't even want to know the kind of shithole he has her staying in.

I play his games, do what he asks of me, and he can't even make sure she's okay? I'm not seething, I'm fucking gone. Ready to tell him to shove all of this up his prick of an ass.

"Ashton, let me talk to Dad again. I'll make sure you get moved back. Don't worry, okay?"

"Okay, sis," she sniffles. "Thanks, and I'm sorry. I love you, you know that, right? You're the only one who ever believed me, who ever cared." A rock of emotion lodges itself in my throat. I can't do this right now. I can't talk about this. Parker thinks his brother is innocent, but would he still think that if he saw my sister's tears. If he heard the agony in her voice. If he knew that she wanted to end her life a thousand times over because the memories from that night haunt her even when she's awake.

"I love you too, and yes, I know you do. Everything is going to be okay," I soothe her like a mother soothes their child. Even though I'm younger than her, somehow, I took over the nurturing role after our mother's death. Ashton lost it, fell off the deep end, and I was the life preserver that kept us both above water.

She hands the phone back to my dad, and as soon as I hear him clearing his throat, I go off on him. "What the hell? Where is she, and why did you move her?"

"Watch your tone, I'm still your father, and I told you how important it is to reinsert yourself into the crowd at Blackthorn.

Business is bad, and I need those contacts. Have you made progress with Parker?"

I close my eyes and pinch the bridge of my nose. I don't know if I call him breaking into my room, scaring the shit out of me, and then kissing me, making progress.

"I'm working on it."

"Great, there is a fundraiser coming up. Parker's father is hosting. I need you to get invited." I don't even think before I speak.

"Move Ashton, and I'll get you an invite."

"I'll move her after the fundraiser. I can't be sure you'll actually get us in."

"No, you need to move her now. I'm telling you right now, I'm getting you an invite. Move her first, then fundraiser." I know I'm playing a dangerous game, but I also know that Ashton is in danger, wherever she is. I need to get her moved as soon as possible.

I hear my father cursing under his breath. "Fine, I'll do it now while I'm here," he finally says.

"Call me when you get to the other place. I want to talk to her again."

"You don't trust my word?"

"Do you really expect me to?"

"Smart girl, Willow. Something might become of you, after all," he taunts before hanging up the phone. *Asshole.*

It takes me a few minutes to realize what I have just done. I promised him an invite. How the hell I'm going to deliver on that, I do not know. All I know is that I have to do it, which means I actually need to talk to Parker. Thinking about our last few encounters, I'm sure that's going to go over well. I don't even know how to get in touch with him besides seeing him in class.

My gaze swings to the clock, hanging on the otherwise bare wall. Shit, biochemistry starts soon. Scrambling off my bed, I quickly get into a pair of jeans and sneakers. Grabbing my bag and sweater on the way, I'm out the door in two minutes.

Speed walking down the stairs and across campus, I make it to the building in under ten minutes. When I look inside the classroom, I notice neither Parker nor his friends are there yet. Leaning against the wall next to the door, I wait for him. The other students who pass me to get inside mostly ignore me, but here and there, I get a nasty look as well, and I wonder what Parker told them about me.

Nervously, I shift my weight back and forth on my legs. When I finally spot him coming around the corner, my nervousness turns into a mixture of excitement and fear. My pulse thunders in my ears, and when he looks up, our eyes lock. Every cell in my body heats, threatening to combust. He looks angelic, but like a wolf in sheep's clothing, he hides his dark side well. I snap out of the trance I'm in when I see a deep frown settle into the hard ridges of his face.

Then he's heading straight for me. Walking with a purpose. His stupid long legs eat up the space separating us.

"Stupid, stupid girl. You don't know when to quit. I thought I specifically told you not to come to class," his voice is piss and vinegar. Reaching me, he gets right in my face, not keeping any personal space between us. I try to back up, but I'm already pressed against the wall.

I'm trapped all over again.

Out of the corner of my eye, I see the professor passing us on his way into the class. Parker is clearly hovering over me in a threatening manner. Doesn't he see that? Oh, wait, he does, and he doesn't care. Dr. Dawson hurries by us and closes the classroom door behind him, proving my statement to be true.

"I know what you said, but I can't just stop going to class. I need to be here, okay? Trust me, I don't want to be here anymore than you want me to be, but I don't have a choice."

Parker lifts a thick brow and places a hand on the wall next to me, caging me in. Having him this close makes it hard for me to think, to breathe. "And why should I care about what you want or need?"

"You don't have to care. I know you hate me and that's fine by me, but I'm not stupid, I know you still want me. Maybe we can come to an arrangement?" Just saying the words makes me feel dirty and cheap. I can call it whatever I want, justify it with the fact that I'm doing this for my sister. But, in the end, I'm doing nothing more than whoring myself out.

"What kind of *arrangement*?" Parker smirks widely, and all I want to do is wipe that smug smile off his face.

"Whatever you want," I shrug. Unable to stand the triumphant look in his eyes any longer, I avert my gaze. Concentrating on some random spot behind Parker, I continue, "Let me stay here, at least this semester."

"What exactly do I get in return?" He sounds seriously intrigued now.

"You know what." He is not seriously going to make me say it, is he?

"I want to hear you say it." Of course, he is. *Please, someone, kill me now.*

"Whatever you want," I repeat, "if you want me to suck you off, I will."

"I want more than you sucking me off. Although, that would be a good start."

"You want to fuck me? Fine, I'll do that too, but I need something else."

"Is that so? It seems you're not really in a position to be asking me for favors." I resist the urge to roll my eyes.

"If you want me to fuck you, *willingly,* then I want an invite to the fundraiser your dad is hosting, on top of being able to stay here for the rest of the semester."

"Hmm...and why do you want an invite?"

I chew on the inside of my cheek until the copper tang of

blood fills my mouth. He is enjoying my misery. Every minute of it.

"It doesn't matter why I want an invite. Can you get me one or not?"

A heavy silence blankets us, and I worry for a second that he might say no. If he does, what the hell am I going to do? Beg, plead? I hate feeling as helpless as I am right now. When he still doesn't say anything after a while, I return my gaze to his face. I find him studying me, his eyes scanning my face for something. What exactly, I don't know.

"Probably," he finally says.

"So, we have a deal?"

"Sure, we have a deal." His eyes basically gleam with excitement. I'm sure he is already conjuring up all kinds of things in his mind.

"What deal?" Warren cuts in, appearing out of nowhere. His eyes glitter with mischief, and he grins at me. When I look up and over his shoulder, I notice Nate strolling behind Warren. Great, the gang is complete. Blackthorn's elite douchebag club.

"I'm going to allow Willow to stay here for now, in exchange for her... well, her body," Parker snickers.

"Sounds like a great deal," Nate chimes in. Reaching out for me, his knuckles graze my cheek. A coldness sweeps through me at his touch. "Think maybe I can get in on this deal?"

I turn my face away from him, hoping to get out of his reach, but before I can move more than an inch, Parker grabs on to Nate's wrist and shoves it away. "You're not part of this. Don't touch what is mine," he growls, and the warning is clear.

"Fine, be a prude. I would have been happy to share," Nate grins and steps back. "Let's go in before we miss the whole class."

Warren nods and opens the door. I wait for Parker to move out of my way, so we can go too, but instead, he grabs my arm and pulls me in the other direction. My feet drag across the floor as I try and root them into the concrete.

"What are you doing?" I choke out, surprised by his actions.

"We're leaving."

"What? To go where?"

"My place," he says, matter of factly.

"Right now?" I should be surprised, but I'm still shocked that it's going to happen so fast. I just decided I was going to do this thirty-minutes ago, and now it's happening.

"I've already missed the last class, I need to be there."

"Don't worry about that class. You'll get an A either way. It's graded by groups, remember." Of course, I'm still part of his group, and naturally, he gets an A, no matter what he does.

He pulls me all the way to the parking lot behind the building. With my much shorter legs, I have a hard time keeping up with his speed, but somehow, manage without tripping. When we get to some expensive-looking sports car, he unlocks the door and opens it for me. Shoving me in the passenger seat, he orders me to buckle up before sprinting around the car and getting into the driver's seat.

What a gentleman.

Apparently, he can't get me to his place fast enough, because as soon as the engine roars to life, we are speeding out of the parking lot. I don't know if I should be scared or flattered by his urgency to get me into bed.

As we drive to his place, I memorize the way just in case I have to walk back to campus. Luckily, the drive only takes five minutes, which means I could walk home, and it wouldn't take me, but half an hour. I'm paranoid, I know, but I'm not going into this situation blind.

I'm surprised when we pull up to a modern but small home. I was expecting something more like a mansion. He parks in the driveway and cuts the engine.

"Come on," he orders as he gets out.

"Sure, but only since you asked so nicely," I say under my breath while getting out of the car. He is already unlocking the front door when I come up behind him. As I follow him inside, the reality of what I'm about to do sets in. He closes the door behind us, and I start to shake slightly.

"Don't look so scared. You're the one who made the offer. If you don't want this, turn around and walk away. Just know I won't let you make me another offer."

I glance at the door, knowing damn well that I can't leave. If I do, Ashton won't get the care she needs, my father will make my life hell. I think about what he said. *Sex is only what you make of it.* It doesn't have to mean anything. Who cares that he'll be my first? No one has to know, not even him.

"No, I want to stay."

Parker smiles so widely his dimples deepen like I've never seen before. "Great, come with me then."

He leads me into the living room, and though I don't mean too, I openly gawk at my surroundings. Just like the outside, the decor inside is modern and clean with a black and gray color scheme. It fits Parker very much.

My gaze skirts from the décor to Parker, who moves like a panther, taking a seat on the black leather couch, looking smug as ever. Resting his arms on the back of the couch, he pins me with his punishing gaze while I just stand there in front of him, unsure of what to do next.

"I..." The word has just passed my wobbling lips when he starts to shake his head.

"Get on your knees, Willow." His voice is suddenly smoother, but also thick, like honey. Is he trying to tame me? Soothe me with his voice? He looks relaxed, almost like he is just lounging, ready to watch a movie. And that would be believable, except for the bulge in his jeans, which tells me that he has other things on his mind.

Part of me wants to ask him what happens if I don't? Will he make me? I suck in a harsh breath, the reminder of the way his lips felt against mine, the fire that consumed me. I wanted him to keep going as much as I wanted to push him away, and I still don't understand why. Why the enemy in all of this tempts me so badly.

"Tick tock, Willow. I'm losing my patience with you," the bite to his tone tells me he's not lying, and I don't want to risk pushing him any more than I already have. Swallowing every ounce of pride I have down, I move toward him. Each step seems to take an eternity, and when I reach him, I drop down to my knees.

My legs wobble, and my stomach churns when I make contact with the cold floor. This is not how I wanted my first blow job to go.

Kneeling between his legs, I brush a few strands of hair that have fallen into my face away, and stare up at him, waiting for him to tell me what to do next. He admires me for a moment like one might admire a piece of art, examining it, determining its worth.

Then without saying a single word, he reaches for the button on his jeans, lifts his hips, pushes the fabric down, and pulls his rock-hard cock free. I couldn't look away even if I wanted to. Thick, and hard as steel, just as I remember.

Parker emits a deep husky chuckle from his chest. "Why are you looking at it like it might kill you?" *Because it might.* The thing is long and thick, and there is no way in hell, it's all going to fit in my mouth.

"I'm not," I muster up the lie, refusing to let him know just how inexperienced I am with all of this.

Licking his lips, he places both his hands behind his head, "I'm waiting, Willow, but soon, I won't wait. Soon I'm going to just take..." He pauses, and his eyes light up with something, something that reminds me of the way a villain gloats when he's defeated his enemy. "Or maybe that's what you want..."

"No..." I shake my head and move my trembling hand to his cock. Exhaling, I tell myself I can do this. *It's just a blow job.* Not rocket science. I bite back a gasp at the softness of his mushroom head, and move my hand lower, till it's wrapped around his shaft. Then I lean forward to suck the tip into my mouth. I keep my eyes on Parker's watching his every move as I do so.

"I want a real fucking blow job, Willow, not some teenage bullshit," he grits out and moves one of his hands into my hair. His fingers splay through the strands, snagging on a few, but that doesn't stop him. He tugs, causing pain to lance across my scalp. Placing my hands on his knees, I'm tempted to pull away, but with pressure on the back of my head, I know it wouldn't do me any good. He has me right where he wants me.

I'm not prepared for what comes next, though.

Holding my head in place, he thrusts his hips upward, and his thick shaft skids to the back of my throat. *Oh, god.* My gag reflex springs to life, and tears form in my eyes at the intrusion. My lungs burn, and I struggle against his hold, trying to pull away. A mumbled whimper vibrates through his cock, and just when I'm sure he's going to try and murder me with the thing, he pulls back, only to do it all over again.

"Fuck, your mouth feels like heaven," he mumbles while I choke around his length. When he pulls back, I suck in a greedy breath of air, saliva dribbling from my bottom lip. He pulls my head down again, and I make a loud, gagging noise as he bottoms out in my throat. Digging my nails into his jean-clad thighs only seems to egg him on, his strokes become more violent, harder.

He is all around me. Invading every one of my senses. All I can feel is him, claiming me. All I can smell is his rich, exotic scent. He's wild and rough, and I know if I let him even a little bit, he'll consume me. He'll snuff out all the good in me.

As he continues to fuck my mouth, giving me only tiny moments to catch my breath, warmth starts to pool in my belly.

Each stroke moves the warmth further south until I can feel the wetness of my arousal against my panties. Being dominated by him turns me on as much as it sickens me.

"Shit, Willow, suck me hard, make me come in that pretty little mouth." The thickness of his voice ripples through me. Oddly, I want to prove myself to him, that I'm stronger than him, that he can't break me. At the same time, I want to disobey him and tell him that I can't do this... I want to run out of this house and never come back.

Tears sting my eyes, the confusion of everything zings through me, appearing in my mind like a bright blinking neon sign. Tugging at my hair, causing my scalp to burn with pain, he bucks his hips a few more times until I feel him pulse deep inside my throat.

So deep that I can barely taste his come. Only when he releases me and his cock slides out, do I notice the saltiness that's left behind on my tongue.

"That was fucking amazing..." Parker sighs and settles back into the couch. His deep brown eyes are closed now, and he looks relaxed like he doesn't have a care in the world. I don't know why, but I remain there for a long moment, just staring at him.

Dread slowly seeps into every pore as I realize what I've just done. I let my gaze move to my hands, and all I can see is dirt on them, my skin forever dirty. I've never felt so disgusted, so tainted in all my life. Even worse, I feel ashamed because deep down, a part of me liked it. Shaking my head, I will the thoughts away. I'm so fucking confused. I don't know what to think right now. What I do know is that I need to get out of here. I need to get away from him.

By the time I manage to get up and stand on unsure legs, I'm doing the one thing I swore to myself I'd never do in front of him... I'm crying. Big fat tears roll down my face, I'm no longer able to keep my emotions in check.

No. I can't. I won't.

Parker's eyes pop open and immediately find mine. Instantly, I look away. I don't want to see how much he enjoys seeing me like this. Breaking down like he always wanted me to. Spinning around on my heels, I run toward the door.

"Willow," he calls out to me, but I don't stop. I can't. I refuse to. Pushing myself, I open the front door and escape the confines of the house. Once outside, I let my feet carry me down the driveway and away from his house. I don't stop running until my lungs burn, begging me to slow down or fall over dead.

This was a mistake, a huge mistake, and one that I'll have to make again if I have even a chance at surviving my father and Parker.

10

PARKER

*E*very thought I have leads me back to her. I can't get the way she looked on her knees, between my legs, with my cock in her mouth out of my head. She looked like a pure, innocent angel with a cracked halo. So fragile and perfect. So fucking breakable.

I'd never come so hard in my entire life. My intentions weren't to just fuck her face, but one dip inside her hot wet mouth, and I lost it. I exploded, and everything faded away. All I could feel was her mouth wrapped around my cock, and it felt like heaven.

It wasn't even her blow job skills that made it good, it was good because it was her, the girl I'd fantasized about since I was fifteen. Frankly, her skills sucked, I don't think she'd given many blow jobs before, maybe not any.

Which only adds to her innocent appeal.

Even though she didn't know what she was doing, everything was perfect. Right until the moment she got up, and I saw the look on her face. I do my best to forget that part, but guilt is gnawing at me like a starving animal gnaws on a carcass. Maybe I took it too far, maybe I should have been a little gentler. I'm confused about my feelings, all I know is that I'll have to control myself better next time.

Next time. Just thinking about it has my cock straining against my jeans. I adjust my crotch before people can notice my hard-on as I walk across campus, then again, no one would dare say anything to me. I could kill someone point-blank right here, and the school would remove the body and pretend it never happened.

I just make it around the corner of the cafeteria when I come to a sudden halt. My hands turn into iron fists, my nails digging painfully into my palm as I take in the scene before me. Willow is sitting at a table, Warren and two of our friends, Cameron and Easton are with her. She is trying to eat something, but Warren is hovering over her, pulling her tray away from her. One hand is on the back of her chair as he takes the seat next to her, pulling her so close that his arm is basically wrapped around her. It reminds me too much of a typical couple... boyfriend and girlfriend. The thought amps up my rage. *Mine. She's mine.*

With my blood reaching boiling point, I march over there like I'm marching onto a battlefield. People move out of the way, and as soon as I'm close enough, I grab Warren's neck from behind and pull him out of his seat.

"What the..." he spins around, fists clenched and ready to fight. When he sees that it's me, he lowers his fist and stares at me in confusion. Doesn't he know not to touch what's mine?

"What the hell are you doing? Only I get to touch her." I release him with a shove. Cameron and Easton snicker at the show I'm giving them.

"Fine," he sighs, holding up his hands like he did nothing wrong. "We were just talking, no reason to have a mental breakdown."

Ha, I'm not dumb. Warren and Nate have both been interested in her since that day in the classroom. Warren was interested from the moment he caught sight of her.

"You should be glad we're friends. Because if we weren't, you would be on the floor right now." Dismissing him, I look past him to where Willow is sitting. She hasn't looked up from her food. Using her fork, she picks at the salad in front of her. *What the fuck?* Her disinterest and lack of response to my presence infuriates me.

Obviously, she needs another reminder, another lesson in who owns her, and this entire fucking school. Without an explanation, I grab her upper arm and pull her out of her chair. She drops the fork in the process, and it flies across the table, landing on the side of her plate with a loud cling. I can feel eyes on us, but don't pay them any attention.

"Hey, I was still eating," she complains, trying to pull her arm free. Her eyes are missing their usual gleam.

"Looked like it, but if you're still hungry, you can eat after," I tell her as I pull her through the cafeteria and out the door. She doesn't even try and fight me, and that adds to my newfound level of annoyance. Where is her fight? Her spirit?

"After what?"

"After I'm done with you." Maintaining my grip on her, I walk her across the courtyard and toward her dorm. I don't have the patience to drive to my place today. I need her, and I need her now. My entire body burns to show her that she is mine, and mine alone. The shit with Warren only made my need to possess her stronger.

By the time we get into the dorm, Willow is panting, her chest rising and falling in rapid successions.

"When I said I would do whatever you wanted, I didn't mean *whenever* you wanted." She pants, trying her best to catch her breath. I fish out the key card from my pocket and unlock her dorm room. She already knows I have a key, so there's no reason for me to hide it anymore.

"Doesn't matter, you made a deal with the devil, and in doing so, you gave yourself to me. That means if I want you to suck me off in the cafeteria in front of a room full of people, then you will." With the door open, I usher her into the room and close it behind us, locking it for good measure. Finally, now that we're alone... it feels like the pressure on my lungs has disappeared. When I'm alone with her... *No.* I shake the thought away. She's nothing, a means to an end.

Turning back to Willow, I give her my undivided attention. She looks nervous, even more nervous than she did yesterday, but she's holding onto her pride, using it as a stepping-stone. With her head held high, she's still too proud to admit how scared she is, even though her body vibrates with the feelings she refuses to submit to.

Beautiful. Fragile. She's glass, and I'm the sledgehammer that's going to come crashing down on her.

"Strip," I order, watching her eyes gleam with hatred for me, but hate isn't the only thing in those green depths of hers. There's a crackling of embers, a slow-building fire, and that makes me feel a little less guilty about what's happening here. It makes me feel like maybe, just maybe, a part of her does want this. And that confuses the fuck out of me.

The bullied shouldn't want the bully.

Forcing myself to look anywhere but at her face, I notice her hands are trembling when she slowly grabs the hem of her shirt and starts to pull it upward, revealing her flat stomach, smooth skin, and bra covered tits.

My mouth waters at the sight, and I stop myself from clearing my throat. In one swift movement, she pulls it over her head and throws it un-ceremoniously onto the floor beside her. While stepping out of her sneakers, she starts to undo the button of her skinny jeans. She unzips them and peels them down her slender legs until they're bunched up around her ankles.

When she straightens up, she steps on one side while pulling her leg out of the other, then she kicks her pants off, flinging them across the room like a bratty child. I can't help it, her careless nature calls to me. She doesn't give a fuck, and while that pisses me off, it excites me, all the same.

"Very sexy move," I smile.

She rolls eyes, "Sorry, if you want sexy moves, you need to go to the strip club."

"Oh, but this is so much better. Now the rest..." I motion with my hands to her still covered tits and pussy.

She visibly swallows, her throat bobbing as she reaches back to unclasp her white lace bra before letting it slide off her arms and down her body. Two glorious pink nipples sitting on two perfectly perky breasts greet me, and I have to fight the urge to close the distance between us and take one into my mouth. The only thing keeping me from doing that is knowing she is about to take off more, and I'm not quite ready to scare her.

Her cheeks flame and she chews on her bottom lip, giving off that innocent vibe once more. It hits me then, right in the chest. Fuck, she can't be a virgin, can she? No, no way. I know I joked about it with Warren, but it can't really be true. Perhaps her nervousness comes from inexperience, but there's no way some lucky bastard hasn't got his dick wet inside her yet.

Dipping her thumbs into the waistband of her cotton panties, she starts pulling them down her legs, giving me a glimpse of her bare pussy as she goes. My mouth waters looking at her glistening folds. Fucking hell. I can't wait to taste her, to be inside of her.

"Happy?" She tries to sound strong and defiant, but I don't miss the tremble in her voice or the panic in her eyes. She's scared, and like the fucked-up asshole I am, her fear only makes me want her more.

I shrug, "Get on the bed. I'll be happier when my cock is

inside of you, making you scream my name loud enough for this entire dorm to know that you're mine."

Shivering, Willow takes a hesitant step toward the bed. Will she try and run? Try and fight me? She was the one that asked for this, the one that came to me and made the deal. Surely, she knows what's to come?

Reaching the tiny twin-size mattress, she crawls up onto it, giving me another view of her pussy. Pink, wet, so fucking tempting. My stomach tightens at the thought of slamming into her, and without even thinking, I take a step toward her.

As if she can sense the beast in me, she rolls over on to her back. Her face pales, and I take another step, and then another until I've reached the edge of the bed.

"You should know that your fear only makes me want you more.

I want to fuck her, sink deep inside her, let the entire world know that she is mine, and mine, a-fucking-lone, but with the way her body is shaking now, and her hands fisting the sheets, I shove that desire down. Her fear turns me on, but this isn't just fear, this is something else, something entirely different, and I'm not ready to fully break her yet.

"You're sick," she croaks, her voice trembling.

My lips tip up at the sides, and I'm sure I look like the monster she portrays me to be, in every way. "Yes, but you like it. You might be scared of me, confused and afraid of what I'll do, but something inside of you enjoys it. Something inside of you clings to the darkness inside of me. We're two drops of paint on a white canvas, and one of us is going to dull out the other's color." Lifting my hands, I bring them to her knees and push them apart. "Will it be me, or you?"

A whimper escapes her mouth as I stare down at her pink folds. Her pussy calls to me, and I want to worship it, suck it, lick it, fuck it. I want to own it like she owns a piece of me.

Wrapping my hand around her ankle, I pull her until her ass is at the edge of the bed.

"If you were just going to take it from me, then why strike a deal?" For a moment, I stand there, staring down at my snow white beauty. Did she think I was going to rape her? The thought shocks me and at the same time, makes me want to laugh.

"I could have anyone I want at this school, Willow. If I wanted pussy, I wouldn't have to rape someone." It's then that she almost visibly sinks into the mattress, her chest not rising and falling as rapidly as it was a minute ago. She thought I was going to hurt her... *really* hurt her. *What the fuck?* Is that what she thinks of me?

"I'm an asshole, a crazy bastard who you should definitely stay away from, but I'm not going to take something you aren't willing to give me."

Her thick lashes brush against her cheek as she watches me with caution, "What are you going to take, then?"

With a honeyed voice, I reply, "Whatever you give me."

Using both hands, I slide them under her thighs and then lift, bending her, so her knees come back toward her chest. A tiny gasp meets my ears, but there isn't a *stop* or *no* that follows the action, so I continue.

"Use your hands and hold your legs back against your chest. If you move, I stop and trust me, you don't want me to stop, I mean it."

Like the good girl she is, she moves one of her arms and wraps it around her knees. With both hands to use, I smile, and gently spread her folds, exposing her tiny little diamond of a clit. My tongue darts out over my bottom lip, and I feel my cock harden to the point of pain.

"Has anyone ever eaten you out?" I ask, even though I'm certain I already know the answer.

"N-no..." She stutters, her voice like silk wrapping around

me. The fact that she's so untouched, so perfect, it drives my obsession for her home. It makes me want to possess every inch of her, destroy all the good. Take and take until there is nothing left.

"Good, I'll be your first and your last. No one touches this pussy, no one. Not even you. Not without permission. Do you understand?"

When she doesn't reply right away, I pinch her clit between two fingers, forcing her attention to me.

"Y-yesss… I understand."

"Good," I whisper hoarsely watching as wetness drips down her thighs. She likes this, likes my control.

Rein it in. Calm down.

Exhaling, I let go of her clit and replace my fingers with my tongue. I flick it against the bud instead and listen as Willow lets out a hitched breath at the contact. It's music to my fucking ears, and I do it again, just for safe measure savoring the salty tang of her on my lips, and tongue.

I'm consumed, completely fucking consumed by her, and I'm afraid of what's going to happen when all of this is over.

"What are you going to do?" she asks her voice piercing through the heavy lustful fog around my head.

"Eat," I answer, and drop down to my knees. Giving her no warning of what's to come. I dive right in like a starved fucking man. Using my fingers, I spread her and start working her clit.

I suck on the tiny nub until Willow starts to squirm, and I feel her juices coat my lips more rapidly. *Delicious.* Without realizing it, she starts to buck her hips, and I flatten my tongue against her clit, letting her fuck my face with her inexperienced humps. I never want this to end, never, and that's a fucking problem because eventually, it will.

Bringing a finger to her entrance, I test the resistance before slipping inside with ease. So goddamn wet and warm. She squeezes around my digit like it's a cock, and I let out an animalistic groan against her clit.

Slowly, I start to finger her cunt, listening as she squirms against the sheets, her other hand thrusts into my hair, and she holds me in place as if she knows exactly what she wants and how to get it. *Fuck yes.* This Willow I can handle, this one that wants me as badly as I want her. In this moment, it's no longer about the hate we share but the pleasure.

Knowing she's close, I pull back and place just enough pressure against her clit with my thumb to hold her at the edge. Then, I add a second finger to the first and start to move again, watching as she stretches to take both of them. It's a tight fit, and I can't fucking wait for my cock to be where my fingers are.

"Parker…" She moans my name, and I look up at her. Rosy cheeks, chest rising and falling as if she's just run a mile. She's beautiful, so beautiful it's fucking tragic.

"Come on my fingers. Gush all that hate you have for me, all over them, show me how much you hate me, baby…" I order, my jaw aching as I grit my teeth and watch as she bows off the bed, arching her chest and pushing her puckered nipples into the air.

"I hate you… I hate you so…" The words cut off, and all I hear is a heady gasp.

Like the end to a symphony, she comes apart, her pussy convulses, and a shudder runs through me at the pleasure. *Mine.* Selfishly, I don't wait for her to come down before I remove my fingers and unbutton my pants.

Standing to my full height, I shove my jeans down and pull my cock out. Fisting it in my hands, I start to stroke, envisioning my hand to be Willow's tight little cunt. I want to fill her with my cock so badly, but she's not ready, I know it.

"Let go of your legs," I order, as my strokes grow faster. Pleasure builds in my balls, each determined stroke getting me closer and closer to the finish line. Willow stares at me innocently, a sleepy look in her eyes as she does as she's told.

Mark her. Claim her. Something screams, and I know if I don't, I'll lose my fucking mind.

"I'm going to come all over you, mark your skin, claim your body. You're mine, Willow. Mine to torment." Stroke. "Mine to hate." Stroke. "Mine to break." Stroke. The pleasure becomes so blinding that I rock off my feet, and like a volcano, I erupt.

Ropes of sticky white come spurt from my cock and onto her snowy skin. *Perfection.* I grit my teeth, squeezing the tip of my cock, becoming mesmerized with each drop of come that lands.

Mine. The word echoes in my mind, playing on repeat. My heartbeat soars into my throat, and as the pleasure inside of me simmers, I'm left reeling.

I know I shouldn't want her like this. I can't want her, but I do. I want all of her. A low rising anger replaces the pleasure, and I release my cock and pull my pants back up.

"Congratulations, you've more than earned your invitation to the charity ball."

Something like relief flickers in her features. "Thank you," she whispers, and I *almost* feel bad for what I'm about to say next.

"However, there is a catch..."

Brows furrowing, she sits up and reaches for the sheet beside her. The action infuriates me, but I don't say anything.

"What do you mean there is a catch? You said you would get me an invite?" Tears start to form in her obsidian green eyes, the color almost like you're looking through water to see it.

"And I did." I button my pants back up and shove my hands into the front of my jeans. "You can go, but you have to go with me."

"But... my father wants to go with me, and I don't..." The

second the words leave her mouth, I find that I'm back to hating her again.

"Your father?" I spit, "You were going to bring your father?" I blink, trying to calm my anger down. I should've seen this coming. I should've known that she had ulterior motives, and I guess, in a way, I did know. I asked her why she needed the invite, and she didn't tell me. My mistake. Shaking my head, I whirl around and head for the door. I've been careless when it comes to her, and I'm not sure when this behavior is going to stop.

If my father knew, if anyone here suspected I was weak for her, the enemy. I don't even want to think about the disappointment.

"Parker..." She calls out to me, but I'm too far gone. I have to get away from her. Everything about her is fucking with my head. Unlocking the door, I walk out, not even bothering to close it behind me.

When will I learn that in this game, every action has a repercussion?

11

WILLOW

I don't know why, but I feel bad. I have no reason to feel this way, he has been using me. Using my body, my image for his psychotic pleasure. I try and maintain the goodness that's left inside me. I'm doing this for Ashton, not for my father, not for Parker, or even myself, everything is for my sister. I can't lose her. She is the only family I have left. I don't count my dad, because there is no love between us. I can't count that relationship as family.

The reminder of my sister makes me feel a little better as I head into the coffee shop just off-campus. Blackthorn is a quaint little town, and there are a bunch of tiny little stores all nestled together like a little village at this shopping center.

Now that I've got the official invite to the fundraiser, I have to go dress shopping, which sucks. I didn't want to go, to begin with, and part of that is because I need to be dressed to my father's specifications.

Walking into Java, the door chimes. The smell of coffee permeates the air and fills my nostrils, and for the first time in a long time, I smile.

My entire world might be falling apart, but at least I still have coffee. As I move through the tiny building, I make my way toward the menu board. I don't realize the girl in front of me is Alice, my now ex-roommate until she turns around.

A frown clouds her face when she sees me. "Hey," she greets, sounding a bit unsure what to say.

"Hey," I respond and try to give a tiny smile. I don't hate her for what she did. I'm not stupid; I know she didn't leave out of her own free will.

"Mhm, I'm sorry, Willow... about leaving, ditching you. I..." She stumbles over her words. "I don't know what to say besides I'm sorr—"

"Let me order my coffee, and we can sit down and talk, okay?" I interrupt her. She gives me a tiny nod and heads to a nearby table while I walk up to order my drink. Five minutes later, I have an iced caramel latte in my hands.

Meandering to the table, I sit in the seat across from her. I don't need her to tell me what happened because I had already assumed that Parker had something to do with it, the day she'd disappeared, but I did think she was a friend. And when she left without even a word, it hurt.

"I'm sorry, Willow." She starts, "I didn't want to leave, but I didn't know what to do. Like I told you, Parker's dad owns the school, and if I went against him." A visible shiver ripples through her. "He threatened me. Parker, I mean. I just—"

"Stop, it's okay. You don't have to apologize. I already assumed that it was him, and I'm not mad that you left."

"You aren't?" Alice perks up, her eyes shining a little brighter now.

"No, I was only upset because it felt like I lost my only friend here. You left, and I had no heads up. Then you've avoided me at all cost, making it impossible for me to talk to you about anything. I was worried..." I take a sip of my drink and try to gather my emotions. I didn't think I would have a chance to talk to her, not after she left.

"I was too, but I knew I couldn't say or do anything, and I was afraid if I talked to you…"

"Look, it's okay. It's done and over with. Do you maybe want to hang out?" I give her a cheerful smile hoping that will ease the tension of this conversation.

"Yeah, I'm just studying, but I miss hanging out with you. What do you want to do?"

I make a sour face. "Well, I have to go dress shopping for that stupid charity ball that Parker's dad is putting on. My father is coming to town for it, and since I hate dress shopping, having you tag along might lessen my hate of it. That is if you want to go?"

Alice's eyes light up at the suggestion. "Did you say shopping? I love shopping. You know what? You just follow along, and I'll find the perfect dress and shoes for you."

Oh boy.

We finish our coffee and talk about the classes we are planning to take together next semester. I don't tell her that I don't even know if I'll be here then, simply because I'm not ready to tell her about the deal I made with Parker. I wonder what she would think of me if she knew that I'm basically whoring myself out to the devil.

I push the thought away before it can take root. I'm not a whore, not considering I'm still a virgin, but what I'm doing makes me feel like one. Plus, with Parker's appetite for me, I don't think I'll be a virgin much longer.

"Should we start shopping?" Alice questions and I realize as I glimpse at the screen of my phone, that we've been sitting here for almost an hour talking.

"Shit, yeah, let's go." I drag myself out of the chair and toward the door.

Alice giggles and follows after me, "It'll be fine, with me by your side, it won't take long to find the perfect dress."

"I know, that's not the problem. I just hate shopping and dresses."

With a sigh, we leave the coffee shop together in search of the perfect dress.

~

WE SPEND about an hour in the first store alone. Alice made me try on a million dresses, but none of those were *the one*, as she put it. And she wasn't lying, she really does love shopping.

As we enter the second store, I have this horrible feeling deep in my gut. I don't know why, but it feels like something bad is going to happen. I do my best to swallow the feeling down as I go through the racks, but then I see *him*.

Warren appears out of thin air like a ghost haunting me. My stomach starts to twist into tight knots. Hiding behind the rack, I peek up over it. I'm half tempted to run out of the store, but then I remember I'm here with Alice, and she's somewhere at the back of the store.

Shit. I'm just going to have to sneak past him and pray that he doesn't see me. Moving slowly, I casually walk behind the racks toward the back. When I'm about twenty feet away, I spot Alice, but she isn't alone. *Parker.* Like a damn cancer, that devil of a man has entered my life, eating and taking every single good thing with him. I'm drowning in all his evil, and I don't know how to swim.

Stopping in my tracks, he smiles at something Alice says, and then as if he can sense me watching him, he locks eyes on me. Dark and piercing, I find it hard to breathe being trapped in his steely gaze. My chest rises and falls, but no air enters my lungs. Why can't I breathe? Why does he have such an effect on me?

Knowing I'm watching him, he leans in closer and whisper's something into her ear, and though his eyes and attention are on me, something that I can only describe as burning jealousy forms in my gut. *Why?* Why am I jealous? It's obvious that's what he wants, but I shouldn't care in the first place. I shouldn't care who he sleeps with or flirts with. *But you do.* A voice nags at the back of my brain. Alice laughs once more and responds to whatever it is that he said.

Fuck him. Fuck this. Sneering at him, I let jealousy guide my next move. Turning on my feet, I'm ready to stomp out of the store, but my steps are cut short because right behind me is Warren. Like an all-American golden boy, he stares at me, his muscular arms crossed over his chest.

"Jealous?" He grins, cocking his head to the side to inspect me.

"No," I lie through my teeth. "I was just leaving." I try to push past him, but he steps in front of me once more. All over again, I feel trapped.

Warren shakes his head, disappointment marring his features, "Aren't you here with Alice? It wouldn't make you a very good friend to just leave her here, now would it?"

Before I can come up with a response, I can hear Parker's voice coming closer. When I look over my shoulder, I find him and Alice walking our way.

"Fancy meeting you here," Parker smiles mischievously. I wouldn't be surprised if this were planned. He probably followed us here, trying to ruin my day with the one friend I have. I want to pull him into the back of the store, wrap my hands around his neck, and strangle him.

"Parker invited us to dinner," Alice announces, and suddenly I wish I had told her the whole story. She probably thinks she is doing me a favor, getting me in Parker's good graces or something. She has no idea that what she's done is lead us straight into hell.

"Oh, great," I say, trying my best to sound sarcastic, I put a smile on my face. It's best not to let him know how much I'm loathing this. This is not part of the deal, but I still need that invite and looking at Alice beaming at me, I'm pretty sure she wants to go anyway.

"We just need to find Willow a dress for the fundraiser gala. Maybe we can meet you after we are done here?"

Please, say yes...

"We can wait," Parker answers right away, his gaze burning into mine. "I'd love to see Willow try on some dresses. Maybe she needs some help zipping up."

"Oh... umm yeah... okay. Let me find some for her to try on," Alice stumbles over her words, clearly confused by Parker's interest in me.

"I guess I'll look too." I go to the closest rack and start picking through them, selecting two that I like.

"You can all stop," Parker suddenly calls out. "I found the perfect one."

Sweet baby Jesus. Turning, I find Parker holding up a bright red dress if you can even call the piece of fabric a dress. It looks like it'll barely cover my asshole.

Shaking my head, I purse my lips and place my hands on my hips. "No, I'm not wearing that. I might as well go naked."

"That's an option too," Parker winks at me. "Try it on, I want to see it on you." I feel compelled to yell at him, throw the dress in his face, and tell him to wear it himself if he likes it so much, but I bite the inside of my cheek instead. I still need that invite to the gala, and that means playing whatever stupid game this is.

"Fine," I growl. Walking by him, I reach for the dress, but he holds it up in the air out of reach, and because I'm much shorter than him, I either have to jump like a dog and try to snatch it, or I do nothing. I chose to do nothing.

"I'll help you put it on."

"I can do it myself," I argue.

"I'll help you put it on," Parker repeats, but his tone is much sharper this time. He's not going to let this go, so I either do this or walk out without a dress, and that's also not an option. With dress in hand, he turns and heads toward the fitting rooms. Like a lost puppy, I follow him, ignoring the questioning look Alice gives me when I pass her.

He walks into the dressing rooms like he owns the place, holding the door open for me to follow. As soon as I get inside, he pins me with his gaze. His eyes gleaming with excitement. I hope he isn't thinking about having sex in here, 'cause that's not going to happen.

"Take your clothes off," he orders roughly. When I don't start to move right away, he adds, "Let's go, I'm hungry." I have to stop myself from rolling my eyes.

Huffing, I start undressing. He's already seen me naked and been all up in my lady parts, so what the hell. No point in trying to hide now. Stripping in the least sexy way I can think of, I let my clothes fall to the floor in a heap.

I can feel his eyes on me, blazing a path of heat over my bare flesh. When I'm down to my panties, he hands me the piece of fabric that's trying to be a dress.

I slip into the canary red number. It's a mini dress and barely covers my ass. Looking in the mirror, I stare at my reflection. The dress is completely backless, and the front has a flowy fabric that dips all the way down to my belly button. The little bit of fabric is held up by a thin gold chain that goes around my neck, only adding to the cheap look of this dress.

Hookers look more flattering than me right now.

My gaze meets Parker's in the mirror. "Perfect. That's the one."

"I'm not wearing this. Everyone will look at me. I'm basically naked."

"Wear it or don't go at all," he gives me an ultimatum. "You said I can do what I want with you. That includes dressing you as I see fit."

His remark stings even though I know it shouldn't. Is that all he sees me as? A doll he can do whatever he wants with?

"What about that whole I'm yours, speech. You're telling me you're okay if people look at *what's yours*?" I know I'm walking on thin ice here, but I'm desperate. I really don't want to wear this... like ever.

Parker's nostrils flare, his eyes darken, and his chest puffs up. I know then that I've hit a nerve, but apparently not the right one. "They can look all they want, but I'm the only one who gets to touch."

I'm losing hope with each second, so I decide to try a different tactic. "Please, Parker..." I plead, batting my eyelashes, but it seems the tiny break in my resolve does nothing to help. In fact, it only encourages the beast inside him.

In a breath, he's got a mammoth of a hand wrapped around my throat, and my body shoved against the wall. I try and swallow, try and breathe, but nothing comes. All I feel is his body pinning mine, the hardness of his cock against my bare thigh. I'm trapped, ensnared in his dark gaze, caught in his web. And for some stupid, unknown reason, my stomach flutters, heat flushing my body, making my core throb.

Wrong, this is wrong.

Leaning into my face, he snarls, "You're above begging and pleading, Willow. You don't want to see me lose it. Do what I say, and maybe, just maybe you'll get out of this unscathed."

He lets go of my throat, and I suck in a sharp breath. I know I should be afraid. Deep down, I should be scared of what he might do to me, but a part of me, this sick and twisted part, is curious to see how far he would go.

"I'll wear the dress, but not because you're telling me too," I snap, and start to tug the fabric off. "I'm wearing it because it's my body. Clearly, it doesn't bother you to have others see what is *not* yours, then maybe this dress is the perfect one, after all."

"Don't push me, Willow," Parker hisses, his face millimeters from my own. I can smell the spiciness of his cologne, feel the heat from his body rolling off of him in waves, and my thoughts swirl, going to places they shouldn't. "Remember, I still get to fuck you, and how you act will determine if that's a pleasant or unpleasant experience. I can be the best lay of your life or the most savage of monsters."

Like a fish plucked out of water, I open my mouth and slam it closed again. Whatever I was planning to say has evaporated into the air. I can't believe the balls of this guy. After everything, he still expects me to sleep with him.

His gaze drifts over me one last time, it's predatory and searing, and I don't dare move a muscle until he opens the door and leaves the dressing room.

"What just happened?" I whisper to myself as I sag against the wall, my heartbeat echoing into my ears.

Parker violated my personal space, made me feel like a cheap whore, and for some strange reason, I liked the way he was talking to me, liked the way he was ready to take from me without notice. What is wrong with me?

Maybe he is right, his darkness does call to me, and maybe I really do like it.

12

PARKER

*I*t wasn't my intention to make her jealous by talking to Alice at the dress store, but I have to admit that I liked it. I like knowing I have that kind of power over her, that even though I treat her like I do, part of her still wants me.

Alice picks out a small Italian place for lunch that's within walking distance of the store we just left. Willow stares down at the ground, the bag from the dress store dangling in her hand. I have to stop myself from thinking about how she looked in that little red dress. She had a point when she said I shouldn't want other people to see her in it. Honestly, I don't, but knowing how uncomfortable she'll be the whole night is well worth my own dislike of sharing her. Anyone can look, but if they touch her. The thought makes me want to smash someone's head in.

Warren and Alice make small talk a few feet ahead of us while I hang back by Willow. I do my best to ignore her presence as if it were that easy. She's already under my skin, integrated into the darkest parts of my mind. When we reach the restaurant, I shove all my thoughts into a tight little box and save them for later.

As soon as we walk into La Strada, the hostess heads

straight to us with a wide grin on her face. Tossing her hair over her shoulder, she basically skips my way while batting her eyelashes at me.

"Hey, guys," she greets, while only looking at me with her fuck me eyes.

"Hi there," I reply, taking her bait. "I've never seen you here. You must be new, 'cause I would definitely remember you."

"Yup, just started." Still ignoring everybody else, she asks, "Will you be dining in today?"

"Yes," I wink, "I will be now, and I'm starving." She giggles like a little schoolgirl, and the sound instantly annoys me.

For the first time, she looks past me, acknowledging the rest of the group. "Table for four?"

Smiling, I say, "Yes, please." The smile I give her is legendary, one that often has the ladies tossing their panties at me.

"Follow me," she chimes, grabbing four menus. She takes us to a booth in the back, and I don't miss how she shakes her hips a little more than necessary. My eyes gravitate to her ass, but it doesn't draw my attention like Willow's does. Still, the fact that I know I can piss Willow off by doing basically nothing is too good of a deal to pass up.

When we reach the table, I purposely touch the waitress's lower back, knowing that'll set Willow right off. To add insult to injury, I lean in and whisper into the shell of her ear, "Thank you."

She giggles again, and I take my seat before she gets any ideas and pulls me into the back room or something. As she skips away, Willow comes into view. Just as I had hoped, she is fuming, steam all but blowing out her ears. Her face is scrunched up into a mask that's a mixture of annoyance, anger, and pure jealousy.

Alice slides into the seat across from me, and Willow tries to sit down next to her, but I stop her, my fingers circling her wrist. "Come sit by me, I won't bite." I wink.

She shoots me a death glare and sighs so loudly, I'm sure the entire restaurant can hear her. Nonetheless, she does as she's told.

"Good girl," I whisper and pat her on the knee.

She starts to pull away, but I give her knee a hard squeeze, refusing to give her an inch of space. Unwrapping her silverware from her napkin, I wouldn't be surprised if she fantasizes about stabbing me with that knife in her hand. The silver gleams in the light, and she looks over to me, the embers of jealousy still bright and red.

"Will you two just go ahead an fuck already?" Warren blurts, completely out of the blue. "The sexual tension is too much to handle. I'm suffocating over here."

"Ha, I would rather fuck you than ever consider sleeping with Parker," Willow answers before I can respond. Without even realizing what I do, my grip on her knee tightens. She cries out in pain, slamming her hand down on the table. Half the restaurant turns to see what's going on, but I drown those people out.

Alice gasps and Warren smirks like a fool, and I feel that inky darkness overtaking me.

"I'd have to be interested in sleeping with you, to begin with, and after your pitiful blow job, I'm not certain you would be worth my time."

Alice's eyes grow to the size of saucers. Obviously, she didn't know what her friend was doing this whole time. Willow turns to me, her lip curled with disdain. I can feel the air around us growing, electrically charged. My fingers burn against her jeans, and I'm tempted to drag her into the bathroom and teach her a fucking lesson.

"If you think you going down on me was much better, you

need to re-evaluate your skill set," Willow snarls, and even through the fog of anger, I can't help but smirk.

"You sounded like you had a pretty good time, considering you were screaming my name. I'm pretty sure the whole dorm can vouch for me."

"So, yeah, why haven't you guys fucked yet?" Warren interrupts, sounding genuinely curious.

Shrugging, I say, "She's not worth the time it would take me to put a condom on."

"He's a lunatic prick who gets off on hurting women, that's why," Willow says through clenched teeth. I know a bad situation when I see one, and with both of us angry right now, there is bound to be some type of bloodshed.

Relax. She's just jealous...don't murder her here.

My jaw clenches, and I'm seconds away from saying something cruel, when the waitress pops up out of nowhere, to take our drink order.

"Hi, what can I..." As if she can sense the hostility, she pauses mid-sentence, her eyes moving over each of us. She takes a step back, and I look up at her, giving her my fakest smile.

"Water, please, and water for the lady next to me as well." She nods, and Alice and Warren order their own drinks a couple seconds later. The table falls into silence, and I move my hand up Willow's leg until it's resting on her thigh. Her anger is visible, her body vibrating with rage that makes my cock hard. Fuck, I want her anger, her pain, all her tears. I want to fuck her till she bleeds. Till she's nothing but a whimpering mess.

Maybe that's exactly what I have to do to show her what happens when she challenges me like this. I have to take. I have to prove a point.

The waitress returns with our drinks a moment later, and we all order. When she disappears from the table, Warren gets out his phone and surfs Facebook while Alice looks wide-eyed between Willow and me. I can only imagine what her mind conjures up, most of it probably spot on.

It doesn't matter to me if Warren and Alice hear what I have to say next because they already know it's going to happen.

Leaning into her ear, I brush the silky strands of black hair off her shoulder. "Tonight, you pay the price for this little stunt. I told you not to tempt me. I warned you, and now the beast is going to come out to play. I hope you're ready, Willow."

Sitting up a little straighter, she twists in her seat, her nose brushing against mine. To anyone else in the restaurant, it would look like we're just a couple innocently kissing, but that isn't the case. We aren't lovers. We aren't even friends. We're just two lost souls looking for something to cling on to.

Coal-black lashes fan against her snowy cheeks. "Make me bleed, and I'll make you bleed in return. Blood for blood, Parker." The seduction in her voice zings straight to my cock, and it takes every fiber in my body not to drag her out of that booth and into some dark corner of the restaurant. I want to hurt her, and I want it now. I want to listen to her as she screams my name and begs me to stop. But above all, I just want her.

Twisting away from me, she directs her attention to Alice, and they start a small conversation about classes they like and don't like. Props to Alice for chatting like she isn't completely uncomfortable and freaked out. I ignore them both and try to keep my cool, barely swallowing down my food once it arrives.

Dinner continues without a hitch, but all I can think about is getting Willow alone and back to my place. When the bill arrives, I take it and pay. Warren follows me up to the front, and I can practically hear the questions he has simply from the way he's looking at me.

"So, you and Willow, huh?"

"No, there is no Willow and me. Not like you think anyway. Just fucking, which hasn't taken place yet, but will as soon as we get back to my place."

Warren rubs his hands together, and his eyes gleam with excitement, "Oh, fuck, I have to hear all about this after it happens. All the details. I want to know if she was a virgin. If you made her bleed."

"You're a sick fuck," I tell him.

"Pot calling the kettle black?" He's got a point there.

"Maybe that's why we're friends. We're both fucked up."

"Probably. So be a friend and tell me if she's any good, 'cause you know maybe once you're done with her..."

Pent up aggression makes me snap, and I grab Warren by the collar of his shirt and pin him to the wall. The word *mine* snarling inside my head.

"She's my toy and my revenge. Touch her, and I'll make sure the next person you stick your cock in gives you something you can't cure with an antibiotic."

Releasing him, I turn around and head back toward the girls.

"If she isn't anything to you, then why are you so territorial over her? Once you have your revenge, she'll become free game to the rest of the male student body, and then what are you going to do? Kick all our asses?" His question isn't a dumb one, but it's one I don't have an answer to yet.

Stopping before we get within earshot of the girls, I say, "I don't know what I'm going to do yet, but what I do know is that she's off-limits until I say otherwise. Touch her, and I'll destroy you."

It's obvious he wants to say something, but like the pussy he is, he tucks his tail between his legs and nods, once again reminding me why my family name is more powerful than his. It's not always about the money, but about the bite behind the bark.

Covering the rest of the distance to the table, I find Alice and Willow whispering to each other, their heads forward as if they're telling each other a secret.

"Ready to go?" I ask, and they both jump back from each other.

"Ugh, yeah. I was just going to take Willow home. We came together and..." I cut Alice off before she can finish what she wants to say. I'll give her a gold star for trying to go against me.

"Nice effort, but Willow has to pay her dues. Now, let's go. I'm impatient, and when I get impatient, I tend to lose it a little bit." I direct my words to Willow, who gives Alice a sad smile. How can she be sad, she knew this was going to happen? I warned her. I told her. Push me and see what happens. Well, she pushed, and I took the bait. Now it's time to reel the fish in.

"Goodnight, Alice," Willow whispers and moves out of the booth. Once standing, she smooths her hands down her jean-clad legs, her green eyes move to the person behind me. *Warren.* Fucking fucker.

"Warren, can you please make sure Alice gets home?"

"Sure thing," Warren tsks, and I reach out, grabbing onto Willow's hand. I tug her into my side and guide us out of the restaurant, wondering if she, too, can feel it.

The calm before the storm.

"Are you ready to play, Willow?" I ask when we reach the car.

Willow doesn't say anything, but she doesn't have to. I know she'll play, even if she doesn't want to.

13

WILLOW

How could I have been so stupid? I let my jealousy rule me, and now I'm in Parker's car headed to his house to give him the last shred of my innocence.

Fear and uncertainty swirl around my gut and I'm seriously considering running as soon as the car stops, but where would I go? If I don't get my dad into that stupid fundraiser this weekend, Ashton will pay the price.

Looking out the window, I try to clear my mind. Maybe it won't be so bad, it's just sex, right? How hard can it be?

All too soon, we pull up to Parker's place. He cuts the engine and gets out of the car without a word. I follow him inside, feeling like I'm walking to my execution. He stops in the living room, looking over his shoulder at me. Grinning, he shakes his head and keeps walking to a cabinet. I wonder what he sees right now. Does he see how nervous I am, see me shaking slightly? Who am I kidding, of course, he does.

I watch him open it and realize it's a liquor cabinet. He takes out two glasses and pours some whiskey into both of them. He downs his drink in one gulp, handing me the second.

"Drink," he orders, but he doesn't have to. I'd gladly drink half of the bottle right now, knowing it will calm my nerves. The amber liquid burns all the way down my throat before settling heavy in my stomach.

The empty glass has barely touched the side table when he grabs my wrist and starts pulling me through the house and into his bedroom.

"Take your clothes off," he tells me as he starts taking his own off. His shirt comes off first, and for a second, I just stand there admiring his chest and abs. This only makes me realize that even though he's seen me naked, I haven't even seen him without a shirt.

"Strip," he says more urgent this time. I spring into action, peeling my clothes off, I pile them on the floor next to me.

When he pulls his jeans and boxers down his muscular legs, his already hard as steel cock springs free, and I can't help but gulp. I remember how he felt inside my mouth, how big he is, and I don't know how the hell he is going to fit inside of me. I guess I'm about to find out.

"Get on the bed, on your hands and knees."

I do as he says, getting on the bed, propped up on my hands and knees. He comes beside me but not getting on the bed with me. I feel exposed and humiliated like a thing he is inspecting.

He lays his hand on my lower back, pushing down slightly, so my back is arched, giving him a better view of my pussy. That same hand runs down over my ass and between my legs, where he finds my already wet folds.

"I knew you were going to be wet. You enjoy this too much. You like being my sex toy, don't you?" Using one finger, he probs at my entrance. "I'm going to fuck you here today." Gathering my juices, he slides his finger up to my other hole. "And here, tomorrow."

"I hate you."

"No, you don't, but you probably will by the time I'm done with you." A shiver runs down my spine, and I'm tempted to beg him to let me turn around. I didn't want my first time to be like this, even if it is *just* sex.

His finger goes back to my entrance, and I can feel how wet I am for him, my arousal coating my thighs. Even as afraid as I am, I still want this. I still want him, and that's not something I can deny, something I can tell myself isn't true. With tenderness I wasn't even aware he had, he pumps in and out of me slowly.

My body quivers at the sensations that build in my core and radiate outward. Fisting the tan sheets, I let the pleasure consume me, and mewl when he adds a second finger stretching me slowly. There's a slight burn and a fullness that follows, but it's nothing compared to the pleasure that's already built up.

"I can't wait to see the way your pussy swallows my cock, each delicious inch sinking deeply inside you."

I shudder, the pleasure mounting with each deep thrust. "P-Parker..." I call out his name, my insides twisting painfully as my orgasm takes me by surprise, slamming into me with the force of an asteroid impact. For one single second, the entire world falls away.

For a moment, I forget everything. What we're doing and how much we hate each other. It doesn't matter right now. All that matters is the way he makes me feel, the way I know deep down, that I make him feel.

Sagging against the sheets, I bask in the afterglow of my release. My chest heaves, and I'm sure I'll never catch my breath.

Parker lands a harsh slap to my ass, and I bite back a yelp at the sting that leaves. "Roll over. I want to see how much you hate me as I claim that tight little pussy."

A nervous knot forms in my throat. This is happening. It's

really happening. I'm giving my virginity to a monster, to a man that I hate, but kind of want, all at the same time.

Rolling over, I find Parker completely naked, his body a magnificent sight. My mouth waters at the sight of his smooth chest, and all the flesh that leads down to his perfectly sculpted ab muscles. Each defined muscle stares back at me, taunting me. I want to reach out and trace his body, paint it like a canvas.

"See something you like?" He gives me a lopsided grin, and for once, there is a softness to his eyes. My lips move all on their own.

"You're beautiful," I respond, knowing that's the last thing he expects to hear. It's probably my hormone-soaked brain that made me say such a stupid thing.

Crawling onto the bed, he pauses above me, his hulking frame casting a shadow above mine. I grip onto the sheets like they can save me from him. I can't breathe. I can't swallow. I'm trapped caught in his heady gaze.

"Will you still find me beautiful when I plow into you, stealing that fragile cherry of yours? Will you not call me the monster you claim I am? When I fuck you until you bleed?"

Something has to be wrong with me because while there is a sniggle of fear that forms in my mind, there is a want that overpowers that fright.

"I'm not a virgin," I lie, and that response is one that I may regret. A devilish grin appears on Parker's lips, and I know for sure that I shouldn't have said that.

"Okay," the word rolls off his tongue as he starts to move again. Situating himself between my legs, he reaches out, pinching my nipple between two fingers. The bite of pain zings through me and straight to my core, stoking the fire that he planted there.

"I've dreamt of this day forever, wondering how good it would be. Wondering *if* it would ever happen. I always thought you were too pure for me, too perfect, but now I see. We're the same shade of black. One of us just hides it a little better than the other."

Twisting my nipple a little harder, I bite into my bottom lip to stifle the cry of pain that his touch brings me. After a moment, he releases his harsh grip on the hard bud, and instead, leans down, his body blanketing mine.

The warmth of his body is one I crave. I feel cold, so cold. His arms come down to cage my face, and his hulking frame forces me to spread my legs wider to accommodate his size. My heart thunders in my chest, and all I can hear is the pulsing of blood in my ears.

With Parker this close, I can see the golden flakes in his eyes, the color that I often dismiss because his eyes always seem so dark, cold, and angry. His jaw clenches, and I gulp when his length brushes against my entrance.

Oh, god. It's happening. I do my best not to clam up, thinking back to all the romance novels I've read.

Balancing all his weight on one arm, he snakes a hand between our bodies, guiding the fat head of his cock to my pussy.

"Wait..." My lips tremble, and Parker pauses, just barely, his muscles quivering as he lifts his darkened gaze to my face.

"Are you having second thoughts?"

Shaking my head, I force my heavy tongue to work, "N...no, not that. Condom?" I don't know why I didn't think of this before. I don't know how many women he's been with or what he's done. God knows I don't want to catch something from him.

His eyes burn into mine, and he licks his lips, the same one I feel compelled to kiss right then. "I've never gone raw with anyone before. I'm clean...are you on birth control?"

I shake my head, "I've never had a reason to be."

"You will now," he smiles, and those black eyes of his glitter with unbridled desire.

Rubbing the head of his cock through my folds, gathering up my arousal, he rubs the blunt head over my clit, back and forth until heat starts to reemerge deep inside my belly. Then he moves back down to my entrance. Staring into his eyes, I exhale and wait for the inevitable to take place. With one thrust of his hips, he's inside, and I can't stop myself. Pain ripples through my core and I grip onto his biceps, my nails sinking into the flesh.

The tiniest of whimpers passes my lips.

I want to mark him, hurt him the way he's hurting me right now.

Blood, for blood.

I've never seen him so focused, so consumed. His obsession, his need for me, is fully on display, and it terrifies me because I can see that there is so much more than hate in those eyes of his. There is compassion, want, need, and maybe even...

Interrupting my thoughts, he grits out through his clenched jaw, "I can feel your pussy trying to push me back out. The resistance against the head of my cock. It's time for you to give me the biggest gift of all."

"Parker..." Exhaling his name on a breath, I swallow down the sting of pain that flutters across my middle as he thrusts all the way inside of me. My nails dig into his skin, making him hiss out, his head tipping back at the feelings rippling through him.

My innocence is gone.

Tears fill my eyes, and I blink them away. I don't want him to see what he's done to me. See how he's destroyed me. Made me crave him and hate him all at once. Baring his teeth, he stills, showing me just a sliver of mercy. I don't know if I should thank him or curse him, but before I can consider either option, he's moving again.

Pulling all the way out, he steals the breath from my lungs when he thrusts forward again.

"Fuck." He buries his face into the crook of my neck while his lips bristle against my throat. My heart beating so fast, I'm almost positive he can hear it.

"Part of me wants to be gentle with you, to fuck you with slow leisurely strokes. But the beast in me, the part that's wanted to possess you since the first day I laid eyes on you, wants to rip and tear. To fuck you hard and fast." Unable to form a response to what he's said, a whimper releases from deep within my throat. Pulling back a little, he stares into my eyes, and I already know which part of him has won out.

Without warning, he thrusts into me, claiming a piece of my fragile beating heart. Like a stone being tossed into a pond, pain rips through me, a scream catching in my throat. Positioning his hips, he fucks without restraint, owning each thrust, forcing me to not only feel but see him as well. I know then, I'll never be able to escape him, never be able to forget the piece that he took.

"You're just as good if not better than I imagined you to be. Tight, warm... so fucking warm." The words skate across my face, and while each thrust is still painful, there is a deep-rooted pleasure blooming beneath it. It builds, each stroke a match lighting the flames until the heat becomes too much, and I'm sure I'll burn alive.

Sweat beads above Parker's dark brow and his eyes focus on mine. He can see the pleasure building, my hips lifting with each punishing thrust.

"I knew you'd love the pain that comes with the pleasure. I knew you'd be my queen." His lips find mine, and he kisses me in a way that speaks volumes of the way he feels for me. Those full lips devour mine, swallowing every cry and whimper.

While he continues his assault on my mouth, he presses his groin deeper into my core. I'm full, so full, and I never want to forget this feeling. Pulling back, he snakes a hand between our bodies, finding my swollen clit and rubs gentle circles against it.

"Oh..." I sigh, my back bowing.

"Come for me, come on my cock, squeeze me so tight that I won't be able to forget the way you felt falling apart around me." The friction and his voice are all I need to ignite the fuse of pleasure, and the long-awaited orgasm zings through me. Like a lightning bolt crossing the night sky. I bare down on his cock, squeezing him so tightly, his eyes roll to the back of his head. The pleasure blinds me for a moment, and I soar through the sky like a bird that's been freed from its cage.

Then I'm floating, and Parker is owning me, thrusting harder, faster. The headboard bounces against the wall, and my body moves against the sheets. It's like he's imbedding himself inside of me. *He's owning you.* A little voice chants.

"I want to come inside you, mark you, claim you, your tight cunt as mine, forever-fucking-mine." His voice is deep, hinging on anger, but his face couldn't be any calmer, and against my better judgment, I nod my head.

"Yes, come inside me," I whisper, not understanding why I need that.

With a roar, his movements halt, and he stares at me deeply, a calmness filling his gaze. His hands are clenched fists beside my head, and his body visibly vibrates with pleasure. How I don't know, but his length seems to grow inside of me, and my eyes widen at the pressure that builds there. And then, I feel it. His sticky seed paints me from the inside out, filling my hole to the brim. I should feel something, knowing that, but I don't.

Instead, my eyes grow heavy, all the day's events hitting me at once. Parker takes a moment to gather his wits, and then he eases out of me. I wince in discomfort but don't say anything as he walks away from the bed, the sound of his feet filling my ears.

He's leaving... he finally got what he wanted. Rolling over, I push the ache between my thighs away. I should leave too, get out of bed, find my clothes and escape before he comes back, but the warmth of the sheets beneath my bare skin feels so nice that as soon as I'm on my side, my eyes fall closed.

I'll just lay here for a second...

One second...

14

PARKER

My legs are heavy as I drag myself to the bathroom, leaving her behind in my bed. I can't believe I just did that. I came inside of her after she told me she wasn't on birth control. What the fuck was I thinking? That's just it. I wasn't, at least not with the right head. I'll have to get her the morning after pill or something of the like. I can't have her getting pregnant. My father would kill me, and while I want to ruin Willow's life, I don't want to ruin mine in the process.

Taking out a washcloth from the linen cabinet, I turn the faucet on and wait till the water is lukewarm. Normally, I wouldn't give two fucks about a chick after sex, but the thought of leaving Willow on the bed after coming inside of her, that doesn't sit well with me. It causes an ache to form in my chest. She's not a whore or a sex toy. She's mine, and I need to cherish her, care for her. With the wet washcloth in hand, I walk back into the bedroom.

Like a moth drawn to a flame, I'm pulled in her direction. I find she is still completely naked, curled up on her side now. When I get closer, I notice that her eyes are closed.

Did she go to sleep?

My suspicion is confirmed when I crawl up onto the bed, and she doesn't move or react in any way. My gaze moves to her face. Her mouth is slightly open, and her breathing has evened out. She looks completely peaceful, and I know damn well that she wouldn't look like this if she were awake right now.

No, she'd be tearing the place apart looking for her clothes while doing everything she could to get away from me. Seeing her like this, I decide I like this side of her more at the moment.

Gripping her by the hip, I roll her onto her back, watching her face to see if she stirs. As gently as I can, I reach between her legs and clean the residue of sex away. She doesn't even stir as I wipe her probably tender pussy with the cloth. When I'm done, I look down and find the once white cloth covered in bright red blood.

Staring at the blood-soaked fabric, the contents of my stomach churns. I knew she was lying. I knew she was a virgin, but it still bothers me. I told myself to pace myself, to go easy on her tonight, but I lost all control as soon as I sunk into her. *Reckless.* That's how she makes me feel. With her, I lose all sense of control.

Disappointment punches me in the fucking gut. I should have been more careful, gentler, even if she didn't deserve that, especially after yet again, lying to me.

Why the hell would she tell me she wasn't a virgin anyway? Did she want me to hurt her? All of these questions are fucking with my head. *She's* fucking with my head. I can't handle this right now.

My hands shake as I throw the messed up cloth onto the hardwood floor in the corner of the room. The cleaning lady can get that tomorrow. Pulling the blanket from the bottom of the bed, I tug it over both of us and settle onto the mattress beside her.

Tucking her into my side, I relish in the sensation of having her in my bed. She fits perfectly into my body, like two missing pieces made to fit together.

At least our bodies are, the rest... fuck, no.

~

I don't know what I expected, but waking up to her being gone, surprisingly, wasn't on the list. Still completely naked, I walk through the house looking for any sign of her, even though I know right away that she is gone. I knew the second I opened my eyes that her presence was missing. How fucked up is that?

The place felt emptier, colder without her, and that revelation pissed me off even more than the fact that she just left. She snuck out without a word or a note. Like what the fuck? The rational part of my brain knows that I should have seen it coming. I shouldn't be mad about it. I mean, what did I expect? How else did I see this morning playing out?

We were hardly going to wake up and enjoy a lovely breakfast together after I took her virginity last night. Something she only gave to me because I blackmailed her into it. Running a hand through my hair, I sigh into the empty house, feeling more alone than I ever have before.

This is so fucked up, so fucking disturbing. It's wrong, I know it, and I know Willow knows it, but I can't stop. I have to make her mine. I have to ensure she sees and feels it.

Walking into the kitchen, I start a pot of coffee, and then jump into the shower, washing away the evidence of last night from my skin. Once rinsed, I hop out and dry off before slipping into my usual jeans and T-shirt.

Pocketing my phone, wallet, and keys, I realize just how late for classes I am. Fuck it. I'm only going to be even later because

I have to stop by the pharmacy before I go to class. The thought reminds me that I was stupid enough to not use a condom last night.

Idiot. Thank fuck Willow was a virgin, so I know she doesn't have shit. She's pure, clean like fresh snow.

Grabbing my coffee, I walk outside and head for my car. On the drive to the pharmacy, I start to think of how this is all going to end. There isn't any happily ever after for us. I can't be with her. Not like I wanted to before.

She put my brother in prison or at least was the last nail in his coffin. I'd lose my father's support, my trust fund, the company. My grip on the steering wheel tightens.

She's the fucking enemy, you idiot. Stop thinking with your cock.

Pulling into the pharmacy parking lot, I run inside and grab the Plan B pill. The girl at the counter doesn't even bat an eye at me as I pay for it. Though if I were a girl, there would be a rumor the size of Texas spread around Blackthorn before I even walked out of the store.

Checking my phone, I head to campus, realizing it's now lunch, and my time to catch Willow in passing is slowly dwindling. I park in the student of deans' spot and climb the steps to the mess hall. Everyone scurries out of my way, and as the cafeteria comes into view, the sound of silverware and dishes clanking together fill the space.

My gaze surveys the area and stops when I spot her dark hair and snow white skin. My chest rises and falls like I've just climbed ten flights of stairs, and my heart is rocketing against my ribs, threatening to escape from my chest.

In the corner of the cafeteria, she sits alone, a book open in front of her. Picking up the little triangle sandwich on her plate, she brings it to her lips to take a bite. No better time than now to make my presence known.

Waltzing over to her, I almost run over some guy in the

process. He gives me a dirty look but doesn't say shit, probably because he knows better. When I'm only a few feet away, she looks up. Our gazes collide, and a cosmic event takes place. Instead of taking a bite, she puts her food back down on her plate and gives me her full attention.

Pulling out the chair next to her, I sit down. "I don't remember telling you it was okay to leave." I know before she even opens her mouth that she's full of piss and vinegar today. Maybe I hadn't fucked her hard enough, after all?

"So, what? I'm supposed to stay at your house now? Like a prisoner?" Her eyes narrow.

I lift both shoulders in a shrug, "You are whatever I tell you to be."

She shakes her head, and the lie rolls of her tongue so well if I didn't know the truth, I might believe it, "I had an early class."

Overcome with anger, I slam my fist onto the table, making her plate and silverware rattle and everybody within a ten-foot radius jump.

"Don't fucking lie to me. All you do is lie. Lie. Lie. Lie. I have your fucking class schedule, or have you forgotten? I know you don't have a class until four."

Tossing her hands into the air, she growls, "What the hell did you expect, Parker? Did you want to wake up while I was cuddled up in your bed?"

Yes, that's exactly what I wanted.

"I wasn't done using you yet. I had plans for you this morning, and you ruined them."

Rolling her eyes, she mumbles, "Sorry, I messed up your *plans*, I'm sore anyway."

Does she think that would stop me? She should know better by now. Her pain is my pleasure.

"Your asshole isn't."

"I hate you."

"So you keep telling me."

"What do you want, Parker? I'm assuming you didn't come all the way here to yell at me about ruining your morning." Her expression is bored, but I know it's a mask. How could she be bored when she was writhing beneath me yesterday.

"Actually, I did. But I also came because I fucked up yesterday, and regardless of how infuriating you are, I fix my mistakes."

Confusion settles into her angelic features, "Don't tell me you are actually apologizing because if you are, I'll eat this plate with my sandwich."

"Why would I apologize? I bought you this," I say. Fishing the morning after pill out of my pocket, I throw it in her lap. Her gaze drops down to the box, and when she looks up at me, I see nothing but pure defiance reflecting back at me.

"I'm not taking that." She throws the box back at me like a small child. I catch it in my hand, half denting the box as my temper rises to new heights.

"Why the fuck not?"

"Everything with hormones in it makes me sick. That's why I'm not on the pill."

"Do you want to be sick or pregnant?" I grit out. Beside what my family would think of it, the thought of her having my baby, it's not an unpleasant one. It would definitely solidify my obsessive need to make her mine, that is, if I didn't strangle her first.

"I'd prefer neither, but that doesn't really matter. I just had my period, so I have nothing to worry about."

"I don't care. I would still rather you take it."

Something in her face changes, almost as if she's pained by whatever she is thinking about. "Don't worry about it, okay. I don't need the pill."

"*Don't worry about it?* You're kidding, right? This is not

something to fucking gamble with, Willow. If something happens. If you do get pregnant, I'm fucked, you're fucked."

The air sizzles, and she snaps like frail rope, "I can't get pregnant, Parker. Can you just stop, please?" The ache in her voice reaches inside of me. Maybe I'm stupid, or maybe I need to clean my ears, but I can't be certain that I just heard her correctly. She's young, healthy from what I can see. Why shouldn't she be able to get pregnant?

"What do you mean?" I ask, my voice dropping to a softness that even shocks me.

Her eyes dart down to her hands, "I have POI... it's very unlikely that I will get pregnant... like ever. So, when I say, don't worry, I mean it. You don't have to worry about me messing with your perfect little future. I won't."

Like a kick to the balls, my stomach starts to ache, the pain radiating outward. Every time I think for a second, I could be nice to her, care for her, show her even an ounce of compassion, she shows me the cold side of her. She shows me that she doesn't really give a fuck about me and reminds me that the feelings I have, though blinded by hate, are completely one-sided.

"Take the pill, don't take the pill. I don't give a fuck. Just get yourself on birth control, because next time I fuck you, it'll be raw too, and with the lies you've already told, I can't trust a fucking word that comes out of your mouth."

"I'm not lying..."

I cut her off with a shake of my head.

"Don't fucking speak. Don't say another fucking word because I am this close," I show her with my fingers, "to losing it with you."

Pissed off beyond measure, I shove out of the chair, listening as it clatters to the floor. I need to get away from her before I do something fucking stupid like wrap my hands around her throat and strangle her. Refusing to look at her, I turn on my heels and stomp out of the cafeteria.

Fuck her. Fuck my feelings. All she is to me is revenge. All she'll ever be is a means to an end. Willow Bradford is nothing.

Even angrier than I was before I got here, I head to my car. No way am I'm going to classes today. I can't even think straight, let alone long enough to focus on a textbook.

Once in my car, with the door shut behind me, I grab my phone from my pocket and search POI on WebMD. I don't actually know why I'm doing it. It doesn't matter. I don't really care. And yet I find my eyes devouring the information on the screen.

Primary ovarian insufficiency, or POI, is a medical condition in which the ovaries stop working normally. Women suffering from POI have a five percent chance of getting pregnant at some point in their lives...

Before I can read any further, I'm interrupted by a loud knocking on my window. I look up and find Warren propped up against my car. Annoyed as fuck, I roll the window down.

"What are you doing? You missed class," he says it like I didn't already know.

"I know, asshole. I've been busy."

Warren grins, his smile bigger than I've ever seen, "Please, do tell, how busy were you? Don't spare any details. I've been dying to know. Were we right? Virgin or not?"

"Go away, Warren." I roll my window back up, watching his face contort into shock. Yeah, that's right. I'm not sharing. Not today, not ever.

Fed up, Warren walks away, and I direct my attention back down to my phone. The screen is black, but I remember the words that were there.

She's not lying...

A war rages inside of me. I want to hate her, and part of me does. I hate her for what she represents, for who she is, but I can't deny the other part of me. The part that's wanted her since we were kids.

Taking my head in my hands, I will myself to fall on one side or the other.

Enemy or lover?

Think of your brother...

She's a liar, she has proven it again and again. So how can I want her? How can this be so damn hard?

15

WILLOW

Like the true gentleman he is, Parker insisted on picking me up before the fundraiser. Which leaves me standing outside in front of the dorms in nothing but a red piece of fabric that is pretending to be a dress.

The wind blows, and I feel it on every inch of my flesh. I taped the thin material right above my nipple, hoping that will be enough to keep it in place. But with my luck, I doubt it. I wonder what my father is going to say when he sees me? Internally, I cringe, and my gaze catches on my pretty much bare legs, minus some red tight workout shorts that I put on underneath, so there won't be any accidental mooning tonight.

The sun is already starting to set, and the air is getting nippy. Crossing my arms, I hug myself, making a feeble attempt to get warm. I should have brought a jacket but figured wearing anything but what Parker told me to wear would get me scolded.

I'm two seconds away from saying *fuck it* and running back upstairs to get something to wear over this when I see Parker's car come around the corner.

As soon as he stops the car, I rush inside. Without greeting him, I pull the door shut and turn up the hot air.

"Don't touch that," he growls, pushing my hand away.

"Maybe if I were wearing some more clothes, I wouldn't be freezing my ass off."

"Don't be a baby, it's not that cold outside."

"Says the guy wearing a tux." I roll my eyes and direct my attention to the trees passing by. I don't want to look at his stupid, handsome face. Especially not when he is wearing that sharp-looking tux. I just won't look at him tonight at all. Let's see how long I can keep that up.

After our conversation yesterday, I would've done anything to miss this stupid dinner, but thoughts of my sister kept me grounded to the present, reminding me of the consequences. There were always consequences.

"You look pretty, in case you were wondering," Parker snorts.

"I wasn't, and I don't. Even pretty, I look like a cheap whore. A pretty whore, that's what I look like, and that's what everyone is going to think I am when I walk into this place."

"I mean, technically, they aren't far from the truth…" It feels like he's stabbed me in the chest with his words. Even for Parker, that's a low blow.

Twisting in my seat, I feel compelled to punch him in the face but settle for a snide comment instead, "I've slept with one person, and if you ask me, he wasn't even that good."

Parker strangles the steering wheel, squeezing it so tightly his knuckles turn white, "You just say that 'cause you have no comparison. If I would ever let you sleep with someone else, you would be a terrible disappointment."

Like every time we talk, his snide comments find a way under my skin. Making me itch with anger that refuses to dissipate until I scratch it.

"*If you would let me?* You do realize that this is only temporary, right? This deal is going to be over soon. After this semester, I'm gone. I guess I'll get my comparison then. I'll write you an email about it if you want. I can title it, one woman, thirty men."

Without warning, Parker slams on the breaks, and I gasp, the seat belt tightening, holding me in place.

"What the hell?" I scream at him, fear zinging through my veins. I'm pretty sure I'm having a mild heart attack.

Parker turns to me then, his eyes darker than I've ever seen them. I'm treading a thin line, close to unleashing the beast.

"You are mine! You are mine now, and you will be mine until I say otherwise." He's vibrating with anger, and the air in the car grows hotter with each passing second. For about three seconds, I just stare at him with my mouth hanging open like a fish out of water.

Then, reality finds me, and I throw my head back and laugh. Holding my belly with my hand, I laugh so hard the whole car shakes.

Barely catching my breath, I say, "Why in the world would I stay here after this semester? Why would I ever stay with you after the way you've treated me? You might be a big deal here, but you're not the ruler of the world. In a few weeks, I will leave this place, and you won't ever be able to touch me again."

I don't know where I'll go or what I'll do about my sister, but I'll figure it out. I'm hoping by that time, she'll be well enough to leave the clinic and come live with me. She has to be because I can't keep doing this. I won't be our father's puppet anymore. I won't be Parker's whore as he now calls me. I need to be me, whoever that person is.

Glancing over at Parker, I find him watching me closely. The look in his eyes has me dumbfounded. For a moment, I could swear that he looks scared. A look I've never seen on him before. As quickly as I noticed it, it goes away. His usual anger replacing it.

With shaking hands, Parker turns his attention back to the road, "I'm going to pretend you didn't just say any of that stupid shit. I'm going to pretend because the alternative is dangerous, and I really, really don't want to have to fucking hurt you. So, I'll give you this one, Willow, but next time. Next time you mouth off or threaten me with leaving, I'll be forced to teach you a lesson. One, you won't forget."

I don't say anything else, knowing there isn't a point. You can't reason with crazy. After a beat, Parker navigates us back onto the road. We arrive at the country club in minutes, our conversation still looming above us.

People are already walking in. Men dressed in tuxes and women dressed in elegant dresses. Watch out party people, a much less elegant dress is about to walk in. "Behave, don't make me have to do something I don't want to." Ha, like he wouldn't want to. The guy is mental, there isn't anything he wouldn't do to me. One more reason to get away as fast as I can.

"I'll behave since you asked so nicely."

He puts the car in park, and I'm already out the door. I can't be in this car with him for another second. The cold air hits my bare skin, and I feel like my whole body is one giant goose-bump. I wrap my arms around myself and try not to shake, just as much as I try to ignore all the stares from people that pass by me.

Looking down at the ground, I pray that no one recognizes me. I should have colored my hair last minute or at least cut it. Did more than make myself look even more like a slut.

My thoughts are interrupted when Parker comes up to me and wraps an arm around my shoulder, tugging me into his side. I want to pull away so badly, but his body heat instantly seeps into my skin, and I can't help but lean into him. Needing him sucks.

"Ready?" He whispers into my ear.

"No, but I doubt that matters to you."

"I guess I could fuck you in the backseat of my car really quick if you're not ready to go inside yet. Might do you good too. Loosen you up a bit."

"Ugh, you're a pig. Let's just go."

Keeping his arm wrapped around me, he guides us inside. I don't think there is a person in this place who doesn't gawk at our entrance. *Great.* I'm going to be the talk of the town. Exactly what Parker wanted, I'm sure.

We enter the club, and it looks as extravagant as you would expect it to. I do my best to look anywhere but at the people that pass by us, which is hard because there are a shit-ton of people. Parker stops walking, and a voice I know all too well pricks at my ears.

"Holy shit," Warren's voice is like razor blades against my skin. I don't want to be noticed, gawked at, or inspected, but here I am like a goddamn alien.

"Stop staring," Parker's clipped tone gives away his agitation.

"If you didn't want people to stare, then maybe you shouldn't have put her in something else. Something that makes her look less like she belongs in a local strip club. High-end strip club," he adds as if not wanting to offend me.

For once, I want to high-five Warren and say thank you, but I'm too distracted by his gorgeous companion.

Peeking up through my lashes, I find a girl with hair the color of gold attached to Warren's arm. She looks as unhappy as I am, and instantly, I feel bad for her. I wonder where he found her. I've never seen her before, and I've never heard him talk about a girl either.

"Who's the girl?" Parker asks the question I'm thinking.

"Oh, shit. Sorry. This is Maja. Don't pay her any attention. I don't." *Ass-fucking-hole.*

"Parker..." I hear a deep voice calling from somewhere in the crowd. Parker turns, and since I'm still tucked into his side, I turn with him, coming face to face with Roger Rothschild.

Yeah, this night just keeps getting better and better.

The moment Parker's father sees me, his face falls and contorts into something that looks like a cross between disgust and disappointment. I should tell him I wouldn't look like this if it weren't for his son, but something tells me Parker wouldn't appreciate that.

The man looks like an older version of Parker, dark hair, dark eyes. It's like I'm getting a glimpse into the future, at what Parker will most likely look like as an old man.

Not wanting to look the way I feel, I straighten my spine and hold my head high. I'm fierce, smart, and strong. I can handle this.

"Hey, Dad," Parker greets his father like I'm not here.

"Son, it's good to see you. When you said she was coming, I didn't realize she would be with you." Just like Parker, he talks like I'm not here at all, and I'm not sure what's more insulting, saying it to my face or acting like I'm not even worthy of being addressed at all.

Parker shrugs, "I didn't think it mattered."

Roger's worn face sours, "Your mother isn't going to be happy about this. You know what her family represents."

"Mom isn't here," Parker brushes his father off completely.

"You know she is going to hear about this from her friends. Hell, she probably already knows." His father eyes me up and down, and I so badly want to drop my gaze, but I don't. *I'm strong. I can do this.* "Jesus, you could have at least made sure she put on an appropriate dress before you brought her here. It's a charity gala, not a whore house."

"Dad, you know that's just how the Bradford women are. Always making themselves look like cheap hookers." Rage burns through me, eating away at any common sense.

"You both are absolutely disgusting," I snarl, wanting to

slap them both so badly, I have to dig my nails into my hand to stop myself from following through. I don't wait for either of them to respond. I don't care what they have to say.

Shrugging out of Parker's hold, I speed walk through the crowd. Without looking back, I know Parker is following me. I can feel him lingering behind me. It's strange, this prickling sensation trails up my back, warning me that he's close, too close. Cutting through the banquet area, I make a beeline for the restrooms but come to a halt when I spot my father.

He's engaging in business, I can see it from a mile away, but I don't care. I want him to know that I'm here. I want him to see what his daughter had to do to get him here. Marching right up to him, I give him the biggest smile I can muster.

"Hello, Daddy," I coo.

As soon as he sees me, his face turns ashen, and he excuses himself, grabbing onto my arm and tugging me into the next room, where a bunch of servers stand with trays.

"What in the hell are you wearing?" His eyes move down my body, and over the very small amount of fabric.

"This is what I had to wear to get you a ticket. This is what I had to become…" Tears sting my eyes, and I will them away. Crying isn't going to fix this. My father has never cared about my tears or my sister's. All he cares about is the next deal, the money in his bank account.

"I said to seduce him, Willow, not disgrace our family name." He shakes his head, disappointment dripping from every word. "It's going to take me forever to convince these companies to sign with me."

"I'm sorry, maybe you can just whore me out to one of them? Maybe that'll make them jump at the chance to sign with you?" Everything happens so fast, one minute I'm seething with anger, and the next my father has his hand raised, an angry scowl on his face.

I flinch, preparing myself for the slap, but it never comes.

Out of nowhere, Parker appears, swooping in like a knight to save the day. In a flash, he grabs my father by the wrist, a vicious look flickering in his eyes.

"Please, tell me you weren't planning to hit her?" He seethes, barely containing his rage as he tosses my father's hand away like a piece of garbage. My father's eyes are so large, they look like they might pop out of his eye sockets.

"I-I was... I wasn't going to hit her," he stumbles over his words and takes a step back. And just like that, I've found my father's single weakness.

"Good because if I ever find out you've touched her in any way, business deals will be the least of your concerns." My heart thuds in my throat, and just when I think he will leave it at the vague threat, he adds, "I will kill you, old man. You got that?"

"Got it," my father whispers. Oh, how the mighty have fallen.

"Good, now get the fuck away from her before I have you thrown out." My father doesn't even say goodbye. He just nods, turns, and disappears into the banquet room, leaving me alone with the second biggest monster I know.

Looking up at Parker, I blink the tears from my eyes and prepare myself to shoulder past him. He might've saved me from my father, but he isn't the hero in this story. Not by a long shot. Exhausted and on the verge of breaking into a million pieces, I take a step toward the back exit.

Parker eyes me curiously, "I hope you aren't planning on going anywhere. It seems you made a mockery out of me in front of my father, obviously, forgetting where you fall in the food chain."

"Parker," I whine, wanting him to just quit with the games for one night. "I've had enough for one day, okay? There is only so much of this that I can handle. I'm not going back in there. I can't..." I literally can't. If he wants me to go back in there, he is going to have to drag me in by my hair. I'm not setting another foot back in that banquet hall of my own free will.

"I wasn't planning on going back in there," he smirks, the devil finally showing his true form. "We're going to have some real fun now."

Oh, peachy.

16

PARKER

With my hand wrapped around her wrist like an iron shackle, I pull her down the long hallway and past the bathrooms. The sound of Willow's shoes echo throughout the corridor.

"Where are we going?" Ignoring her, I continue walking. "Parker, slow down. I'm wearing heels," she complains, her breathing ragged. Frustration coats my insides, and the second we get around the corner, I bend down and pick her up, throwing her over my shoulder like a fucking caveman.

"Parker," she gasps, but I ignore her complaint and keep walking until I reach the door leading to the inside pool area. Stepping inside, I kick the door shut behind us. It closes with a heavy thud, and I turn, placing her down on one of the lounge chairs beside the water. For one brief moment, I stare down at her.

She is genuinely beautiful, even in the tacky dress she's wearing, but I don't plan to tell her that. I don't plan to do anything but make sure she understands where she lands on my pole of importance.

"I would tell you to take off your clothes, but you're pretty much already naked," I give her an amused grin.

"Funny..."

"It's one of my best attributes."

She snorts at my response, and I lean down to start peeling off the little piece of fabric covering her body. I want her naked. Like two minutes ago.

"Ouch, that's taped to my skin," she swats my hand away, giving me a dirty look and carefully starts peeling off the double-sided tape. As she pulls the tape off, she says, "Now, I'm definitely not going back in there, and nowhere else for that matter."

Normally, I would disagree with her, just to piss her off, but for once, I can't, because despite what I said before, I hated people looking at her today. Next time, I'll put her in a snowsuit, and make up some horrendous rumor. I don't fucking care if it's a hundred degrees outside. Nobody gets to see what is mine.

Slowly her dress comes off, revealing some hot shorts that were hidden underneath. They match the dress's bright red color.

"Sexy, you wear that so I couldn't show you off to my friends?"

"No, Parker. I wore it so no one would see my vagina or my ass by accident."

"Good girl, protecting my favorite assets."

Her response is to roll her eyes, and I can't lie, all of her back talk is making me harder than steel. She's grown quite a backbone, and I'm ready to snap it. Without having to be told, she shimmies out of those too until she has them around her ankles. I take her high heels off for her, and set them on the floor, before pulling the shorts off the last few inches.

While I work on taking my own clothes off, I take a moment

to admire her perfect body. Smooth white unblemished skin, a soft tummy with a little curve to her hips. She's like an angel, an angel with a halo made of thorns.

"Spread your legs and start playing with yourself. I want you good and wet because I'm going to fuck you fast and hard, and I don't have the patience for foreplay tonight."

I watch her shutter, but I know it's not in fear. I know because even in the dim light, I can see her pussy glistening as soon as she spreads her legs wide for me. I'm already hard as steel by the time I kick my dress pants off. When we're like this, and it's just the two of us, something overcomes me. It's like in the instances where we're both naked and bare, we're the same, equal.

Her slender fingers tentatively find her center. As if she has never touched herself like this before, she starts to gently rub her little nub. Her movements are slow and jerky, and my need for her heightens, mixing with impatience. I've wanted to fuck her since I pulled the car over on the side of the road.

"Don't tell me you've never made yourself come."

Her cheeks turn a subtle tone of pink all the way up to her hairline. "I have, but not like this. Not with someone watching. Plus, we're in a public place. What if someone walks in?"

She should know me by now. I don't care who is there, or what they're doing. If I want a piece of her, I'll take it.

"Then I fuck you in front of them. I don't really see the problem."

"Of course, you don't," she mouths off, rolling her eyes at me at the same time. I decide then that I'm done waiting. Done giving her a chance. Now, I'm going to take, and she's going to give to me because that's how we work. Grabbing her by the wrist, I drag her over to one of the glass patio tables. I can see a visible chill make its way down her spine as I maneuver her, so she is in front of me, her back to my front.

"What are you doing?" She squeaks as I drag my fingers up her spine.

Brushing the hair off of one shoulder, I flick my tongue against her earlobe, smiling at the loud intake of breath, "Fucking the defiance out of you."

Trailing my fingers back up her spine, I grabbed her by the back of the neck and bend her over, until her cheek rests against the cold glass. She gasps as her chest makes contact with the glass, her puckered nipples growing harder.

"Parker," she whines, struggling against my hold. With her ass out and my hand at the back of her neck holding her in place, I feel like I'm the king of her world, and in a way, I guess I am. No one will ever take my place. No one will ever fuck her like I do.

She is mine...all mine.

Using my other hand, I slide the velvety head of my cock up and down her ass crack, contemplating which hole I should take.

"Which hole should I take, Willow? Your tight puckered, asshole looks very ripe and ready for me."

Like a stallion refusing to be tamed, she bucks against me, "No, please, not tonight. I'm not ready..." The fear in her voice makes me harder, and even though she claims not to be ready, I'm half tempted to take it anyway. Every hole on her body is mine. Mine to fuck. Mine to claim.

Sighing, I decide to punish her later, and instead, move the head of my cock to her glistening pussy. Instantly, she calms down, her entire body becoming molten liquid in my hands.

"I shouldn't take mercy on you. Not after the way you acted tonight. But I'm feeling generous. Don't make me regret it." Pushing inside her, I don't stop until my balls rest against her ass. The air in my lungs stills, and stars appear before my eyes. Tight like a glove, the muscles of her pussy quiver around me.

Home. That's what she is to me. Letting go of my restraint, I decide to show her a sliver of the beast hidden beneath the man. Pulling all the way out, I slam back in, listening as she whimpers against the glass, and my skin slaps against hers. There is no comparison to Willow, no woman before her, no woman after her.

My fingers flex against her neck, and I squeeze harder as my thrusts grow harsher.

"Parker," she calls my name on a moan, and I swear, it's like fucking heaven hearing her say my name in such a sexy tone.

"You want to come, don't you? Come all over my cock?" I piston my hips faster, an overwhelming need to please her burning through my veins. I want to feel her erupt, feel her go off like a fucking rocket into the sky. I want her juices to coat my cock, her tiny little pussy to try and push me out.

"Oh, god, yes... yes, please..." She pants, and I wish I could see her face right now. Gritting my teeth, I watch as her pussy swallows my cock. Inch after inch, she takes like she was made for me.

"I'm going to come in this tight little pussy... I want you to come with me." The table scrapes against the floor with each thrust, and Willow starts to arch into me, taking each thrust deeper into her channel.

Like a crazed man, I release her neck and move my hand into her hair, fisting the silky strands, bending her to my will, so she's half arched off the table, with my cock still deep inside of her. *Mine to bend, to break.*

"So, fucking pretty and perfect. My fucking slut. My pussy." I growl into her ear as I pull her flush to my chest and continue to fuck her. My free hand finds her nipple, and I twist hard, wanting to give her a bite of pain with the pleasure.

She lets out a hitched breath, and it must be what she needed because in seconds she starts to go off, her entire body shaking as her pussy contracts around my cock, squeezing me so tightly, I can barely move inside of her. Pleasure barrels down into the bottom of my spine. It pulses outward, making it hard for me to breathe, to do anything. It engulfs me, tugging the come right out of me.

"Fuck, Willow," I grind out as I empty myself inside her, wishing that we could stay like this forever. Her pussy continues to quiver as I come, almost as if it's swallowing every little drop of my release.

Like feathers, we drift down from the high together. Easing out of her, I place a gentle kiss to her shoulder blade. Perfection. That's what we are. When I'm inside her, the entire world fades away. All our problems are gone. I want that. I want Willow, and that's a hard pill for me to swallow. Wanting her is wrong because she represents everything bad that has happened to my family in the last two years. But giving her up means some other bastard gets to have her, and I don't know if I can do that either.

Pulling my dress slacks back on, I put myself away and button up. Then I grab a towel from the pool towel stand and walk over to Willow, who is still partly resting against the glass table. Spreading her legs gently, I clean her like I did the first time, and help her into her dress. She doesn't say anything to me as I do, and in a way, I'm thankful for that.

Silence is what I need right now. There are too many thoughts and emotions swirling around in my head.

When she's covered the best we can manage, I take her hand and head back toward the banquet hall. Willow doesn't say a word, but I know she wants to complain. I don't plan to stay long, just need to tell my father I'm leaving and then I'm out.

As soon as we enter the room, I can feel eyes on us. I'm about to turn to one of the waiters and ask him to find my father when out of thin air, he walks into the room.

"Goodness, Parker," he greets, a frown on his lips when he

sees Willow standing beside me. "Please get her out of here. There is already talk, and I don't need our family reputation ruined any more than it already is. I told you revenge was fine, but then you parade her around here like..."

"She's with me, she's not doing anything wrong." I feel each word in my chest, thumping with the beat of my heart. Bringing her here, dressed like this... it was for revenge, yes, but I didn't expect so much shit to be tossed on Willow. Her father trying to hit her, my father calling her a whore in front of anyone that was within earshot. Guilt gnaws at my insides. I can feel the wall coming back up around her, feel her tugging her hand out of my own.

"No need to defend me, Parker. We all know that I'm a liar, and well," she gestures to her dress, "now a whore. I think it's time I go back to the corner." Turning to face her, I burn to take her across my knee and spank some sense into her. I don't understand the feelings I'm having.

"Thank you," my father smiles, and Willow takes a step away from me. A coldness sweeps through my body at the loss of her body contact.

"You don't have to leave," I tell her.

"Yes, she does, son. I need to have a word with you, anyway. Goodnight," my father, makes a *shoo* gesture to her, and I grind my teeth together to stop myself from lashing out at the asshole. The only one who gets to be a dick to her is me. She's mine. Mine to hurt. Mine to fuck. Mine to lov—. I don't finish the thought... there is no way, no fucking way, I'm falling that deep.

Willow chooses then to walk away. My tongue heavy with unsaid words as her heels click against the floor.

Once out of earshot, my father leans in and grabs my shoulder, "Whatever your obsession with her is, end it. I need at least one son that can keep it together. Don't fall for her antics. She's just like her sister... a liar, a slut."

And while she may be a Bradford, I'm slowly starting to find out she's nothing like her sister. Nothing like anything I expected her to be.

17

WILLOW

Giving the cab driver a hefty tip for getting me so quickly, I get out of the car, wishing him a great night. Walking a little bit faster than normal, I head toward the dorm entrance. I can't wait to get inside and take this dress off. I'm going to burn this hideous thing tomorrow, but tonight, all I want to do is take a hot shower and crawl into my bed.

Getting the key card out of my clutch, I arrive at the door, unlocking it with a swipe. I step inside, my high heels clacking on the linoleum floor twice when I hear something move behind me.

I start to twist around, but I only get to turn halfway before someone slams into me. I yelp out in surprise and pain, the sound echoing through the entrance hall. I lose my balance and stagger back, landing on the unforgiving floor with a thud. Pain radiates from my ass and up my spine, making me groan.

That pain is quickly forgotten as I realize what is happening. Looking up, I meet Nate's glassy eyes, his lips pulled back in an angry snarl as if it's my fault he ran me over. If I had to describe him in one word right now, it would be unhinged.

Hating You

There is something about him that seems almost insane. Like it doesn't matter what I say, he will hurt me.

Panic bubbles up inside of me as I scramble back on the floor, trying to put as much distance between us as I can manage. One of my shoes came off during my fall, and I kick the second one off as I scoot back on my ass, knowing that I'm probably going to have to run soon. At least, I hope that I get a chance to.

"You look like a slut," he slurs. His gaze licking my body, and now more than ever, do I cruse Parker for making me wear this.

"What do you want, Nate?"

"I want you to suck my cock. How much do you charge?" An evil grin spreads across his face. "Or is the first one free?"

"I'm not going to do that…"

"Why, you think you're too good for me? That's what your sister thought too." What he says confuses me, but I'm too scared to think about it at the moment. All I want to do is make him go away and lock myself in my dorm.

"I don't think that. Nate, I like you," I lie, "but Parker would be furious if I did anything with you."

That seems to hit a nerve, and instead of calming the situation, it escalates it. The tiny hairs on the back of my neck stand on end.

"I don't fucking care what the golden boy thinks," he growls, anger coming off of him in waves.

Next thing I know, he's lunging for me, but I was already expecting it. Adrenaline floods my body, helping me to move quickly and efficiently. In a flash, I'm up and running down the hallway before he even realizes what's going on. He might be bigger and stronger, but he is also drunk. I can smell it and see it from a mile away. Somewhere behind me, he starts to stagger.

My bare feet pound against the cold floor as I run down the dark, empty corridor leading to the laundry rooms. I hear Nate following behind me, but the distance between us is growing. My heart pounds so viciously, I worry it might explode. I contemplate screaming for help, but I doubt that anyone would hear me, and if they do, would they help? I decide my best bet is to get away and hide.

As if Nate can read my mind, he roars behind me like an angry bear, "You can't get away. Your sister ran, and I caught her too." *What did he just say?* His words hit me at a hundred miles per hour, slamming into me and knocking me to the ground. The first comment I had pushed away, but I can't ignore his second statement.

It can't be... he didn't...

I want to stop running, turn around, and demand he tell me what the hell it is he's talking about, but my survival instincts won't let me. A throbbing at the back of my head tells me to keep running, to hide. Taking a sharp corner, I hear a loud thud, followed by a string of curses behind me. Nate must've fallen, that's my chance. *Hide.* Instead of continuing forward with my run, I dash around the back staircase and hide in a dark corner beneath it. My entire body shakes as I pull my legs to my chest and squeeze myself into the tiny-ass corner. I've just gotten situated when the sound of his heavy footfalls get closer.

I clamp my shaking hand over my mouth to keep myself from making a noise. This hiding idea could seriously backfire. If he finds me here in this dark corner, I might not get out of here alive, and even if I do, I'll have a scar that no one can see, just like my sister.

"Oh, Willow, come out and play with me, will ya? No reason to hide. I just want some fun. If you behave, I'll make it good for you. Your sister didn't behave, so I had to rough her up a little, but that was her own fault."

No, no... It can't be. I saw him. I saw Brett. There was DNA evidence. It had to have been him. Ashton told me, and the jacket, the rape kit. It can't be. There isn't a way. Confusion and fear slither through my insides like a snake.

The air around me grows heavy, my chest rising and falling so rapidly I'm afraid I might give myself away.

Like a bull, Nate grows more agitated. "You stupid, bitch! Come out!" He yells through the building, loud enough for hope to bloom inside of me. Someone might hear him, even though most rooms are upstairs and not on this floor, someone must hear. Maybe they'll call campus police? Maybe they'll...

"I'm going to fuck you up when I find you. I'm going to make you bleed. You'll be begging me to stop."

My whole body shivers, and I have to clench my teeth so they won't rattle together. Swallowing down a whimper, I say a silent prayer in my head.

"When I'm done with you, I'll send you in a box to your boyfriend. Maybe that will teach him that he isn't god."

Please don't let him find me.

My heart stops, and all the air leaves my lungs when my phone vibrates in my bra. It's on vibrate only, but even that sounds like a freaking air horn in the otherwise silent space. I completely forgot that I even had it with me.

I fish it out of my bra as fast as I can without making another sound. I look at the bright screen to find Parker has sent me a text message. I don't even read it. All I do is unlock the screen, find Parker's name from my recent call list, and hit the green button.

"P-parker..." I whisper into the receiver as soon as I hear him pick up.

"Willow? What's wrong?" His voice is instantly on edge, wrapped up in concern and a hint of panic. He has no idea. Not yet.

"N-Nate," I say almost silently. "He is... he is..." I can't even get the words out. I feel like there is a thick chain wrapped around my throat, tightening with each breath I take.

"Where are you? Are you at the dorms?" While he asks, I can already hear the engine of his car revving up in the background.

"Yes, under the back stairs."

"Stay hidden, don't move. Don't make a sound," he tells me as if I would do anything else. The phone goes dead, and I listen for Nate, hoping he is still going in the other direction. I hold my breath, straining my ears to take in any sound.

"I know you are still here. Come out, slut!" His voice is coming closer again, but he must not know exactly where I am, and that's my only saving grace right now. It should only take Parker five minutes to get here, but a lot can happen in five minutes. I try not to think about that, and instead will Parker to get here faster.

"You're a fucking tease, you know that? Just wait till I find you," he threatens, making my stomach churn. Squeezing my eyes shut, I wrap my arms around myself, wishing I could just disappear. Wishing I could be sucked into the concrete behind me, protected and safe. Then like the calm before the storm, silence blankets me. I strain to hear anything, anything at all.

He is still here, but not moving. What is he doing? The sound of a door being kicked in pierces through the air, and my whole body jerks. The phone slips from my fingers and lands on the floor with a loud clash. *Shit!*

"Oh, you stupid, bitch. I found you," he laughs and heads toward me. With every step closer, my heart starts beating faster. Tears start running down my cheeks, and I feel like I might throw up any minute now.

"Nate!" Parker's voice cuts through the air, and I take in a sharp breath, both in relief and in terror. What if Nate has a weapon, what if he hurts Parker? Oh, god. Panic circles me like a shark in blood-filled water.

"Fucking shit," Nate curses, and the next thing I can hear is the retreating of his footsteps.

"Willow," Parker calls out for me, his voice coming closer now. I'm still so terrified that I can't get a word out, even knowing that it's probably safe now.

"Willow," Parker's voice wraps around me like a thick wool blanket on a winter's day. A moment later, he appears in front of me. Like a freaking avenging angel, he stands before me, tall and strong. As soon as I see him, I start sobbing. He squats down in front of me and opens his arms to me.

He almost got me. He almost hurt me.

I'm crying so hard now that he is nothing more than a blurry mess.

"Shh, come here," Parker soothes, his voice so velvety and calm, he almost sounds like a different person.

Untangling my own limbs, I crawl out of the corner and throw myself into his arms. He pulls me to his chest, and my sobbing only intensifies.

"It's okay, you are safe. No one will hurt you," he whispers sweet nothings into my hair as he strokes my back. Up and down, up and down. His touch is tender, gentler than I've ever felt.

"Did you call the police?" he asks after a moment.

"No," I manage to say. Only then does it dawn on me. *Why didn't I call the cops?* I was so scared, I thought Nate was going to rape me, beat me, and kill me. I had a phone, but I only called one person. *Parker.* The realization of that settles deep in my gut. What does that mean? Why did I call him when I should've called the cops?

"Why didn't you?"

"I don't know." And truly, I don't. I don't understand.

"Okay, let's get you upstairs," Parker coos. "We'll talk more then."

"Will you stay with me?" No way can I be alone right now.

"Of course." Parker half carries me, holding up most of my weight as we climb the flight of stairs up to my room. We picked up my clutch and shoes on the way. Once we are in the room, I head straight for my bed, crawling under the blanket, and curl up in the fetal position.

Parker slides in a moment later, pulling me to his body. His warmth engulfs me, and I know I'm safe, for now.

Cupping me by the cheek, we stare at each other. The moment is intimate and makes me feel closer to him than I ever have before. "What happened?"

Then it hits me. All at once, I realize just how wrong I was. That I really did screw this up, that I really did hurt an innocent person. "Oh, my god, Parker. Nate... he told me that he did it. He told me he was the one who hurt my sister."

"What?" Parker growls into my face, his whole body tensing, his eyes growing dark, and for a moment, I think he is going to get up, yell at me, maybe even hurt me himself. After all, I'm the reason his brother is in prison right now. I testified against him, helped put him there, though now, it's obvious it was a lie. Brett is innocent and Nate... I shiver.

"I swear, Parker, I thought it was Brett, I saw him... and my sister together, and she swore it was him. I had no reason to doubt her. Why would she lie? Why would anybody lie about this? I-I just don't understand. Nothing makes sense."

Every time I think I calm down a little, my sobbing and shaking intensifies again. To my utter shock, Parker holds me closer, instead of pushing me away. It's like he knows how much I need him, how broken and alone I am.

"Shh, we'll figure it out. Everything is going to be okay. I'm here. I've got you."

For the first time ever, I completely give myself over to him. I have never been so vulnerable and bare before him. I feel raw, all my walls are down. He holds my fragile heart in the palm of his hand, and I can't help but wonder if he knows that too. Does he know that right now, he could crush my soul with the smallest touch?

18

PARKER

She lied. Maybe not of her own volition, but by omission. As I lie in her bed, listening to her snoring softly, I can't help but wonder where that leaves us. My brother is innocent, which I always knew. He'll finally be free, but only after sitting in jail for two years. I should be throttling Willow, telling her that I always knew she was a liar, but instead of feeling angry, I'm sad.

Sad for my brother, sad for Willow, and as pitiful as it might sound, sad for myself. I check the time and read what I'm sending my father over again. It's three o'clock in the morning when I hit send. I know he won't care what time it is. Next, I email our lawyers, they might care what time it is, but we pay them well enough for it not to matter.

Time ticks by at the slowest pace ever, and no matter how many times I close my eyes, I can't fall asleep. My mind is running a million miles a minute, without an end in sight. All I can think about is getting Brett out.

At six in the morning, my phone dings with an email from my father, telling me that everything is set to go. For some reason, my stomach tightens, maybe with fear, or nervousness,

I don't know. Willow hasn't moved next to me, and because I haven't been able to sleep, I've spent most of the night watching her sleep like a creeper.

After a short while, I decide it's time to wake her up. I don't want to surprise her when everyone shows up, and she hasn't even had a chance to open her eyes.

"Willow," I whisper in her ear and start to rub her arm tenderly. "It's time to wake up."

She sucks in a breath and curls deeper into my side. As much as I would love to stay in bed with her all day, fuck, all week, I can't. This needs to be done as fast as possible. When Willow's eyes start to drift closed again, I shake her a little more.

"Hey, I need you to wake up. The police and a lawyer are coming by soon."

"What?" Her voice is raspy and wrapped up in sleep, but she stirs in my arms. Turning so she can see my face, she asks again. "What?"

"My brother's lawyer is coming by; the detectives will be here shortly after that. You need to tell them what happened last night."

"O-okay," she whispers, her eyes darting around the room. "Do I have time to take a shower?"

"Yeah, go ahead." I watch her get up, half tempted to follow her into the shower, but I end up letting her go alone. Less than ten minutes later, she reappears from the bathroom. Her naked body is wrapped up in a towel, beads of water glisten against her bare shoulders. Her black hair seems even darker and falls off her shoulders in large curls. Even freshly showered, she looks like a goddess.

She doesn't even blink as she drops the towel and pulls her panties up her legs. Averting my gaze, I look down at the mattress because if I stare at her for another second, I might just take her against the bed. When I look back up, she's just pulling her shirt over her head.

Crawling back onto the bed, she takes the open spot next to me.

"What happens now?" She whispers, and I can feel how fragile she is, simply by the tone of her voice, almost as if she's given up. I don't want her broken, but I can't do anything to fix her until we fix what's already happened. Nate will pay for fucking with her. I'll personally dish out his ass-kicking and then some.

"Do you know where Ashton is?" I ask, keeping my voice soft.

Her beautiful green eyes fill with rapidly rising fear, "Parker..." She shakes her head, "Please don't make me tell you. What are you going to do to her?" Her panic is palpable, and I can taste it on my tongue.

Cupping her by the cheek, I lean into her, inhaling her sweet scent into my lungs. "The lawyers and detectives are going to want to talk to her. We're not going to do anything to her. Just talk." I don't know how I'm remaining so calm right now, but what I do know is that if I start to break down, Willow will clamp up, and I need her to be open if I'm going to get my brother out of this fucking mess.

"Parker," she pleads, her fingers gripping onto my arm, "she's incredibly fragile right now. Please don't do this. Won't it be enough if I say what Nate told me?" I know what she's feeling right now, the need to protect her family and her sibling. But I can't, *won't* let this go on any longer. Brett is innocent, and he's spent enough time paying for another man's crime.

I shake my head, trying to keep my cool, "I've been emailing back and forth with the lawyer all morning. What happened yesterday will reopen an investigation, but it won't help get my brother out any time soon. There is too much evidence against him."

"Okay," she whimpers, and I can see the indecision on her face. If she doesn't tell me. Fuck, I don't even want to think about it. "You're right. We need to do this as quickly as possible…. Ashton is… she is in a rehab facility. She is in a bad place. Has been since that night. She's tried to kill herself twice." Willow's voice breaks at the end, and like an overflowing sink, the emotion inside her spills over. She lets her face fall into her hands and starts crying again.

Shit. I didn't know Ashton was doing that bad. I've hated her for so long for putting my brother in prison. It was easy to imagine that she was somewhere out there, living a good life, while my brother was rotting in jail. The thought used to make my anger grow, and I fed off that anger for so long. If I'm honest with myself, I wanted to feed it. I wanted that fury to grow because it was the only thing I had left. I let it fester like a wound that would never heal. For the first time in two years, I let my empathy take over as I think about poor Ashton, and what she has been through. She's suffered so much. I can't even imagine.

"We'll make sure that whoever questions her is trained to talk to victims of assault," I try and soothe her. My phone rings in my pocket while I'm talking, but I ignore it knowing already who it is.

"The lawyer is here," I tell Willow after I check my phone.

Her face turns sickly pale, fear bubbling to the surface, "Will you be able to stay? I don't want to be alone with someone I don't know."

"I'm sure it's okay if I stay." I give her a reassuring smile, and then press my lips to her forehead before getting up to open the door for the lawyer. I can't help but notice how she is clinging onto me for support. How she needs me and wants me right now. I hate the circumstances, but I do not hate this new side of her. I don't hate it at all. In fact, it makes me crave her that much more, and I'm not sure I've ever been more terrified of the unknown and what the future holds than right now.

～

It takes two hours for them to take her statement and get all the paperwork taken care of. Before they leave, the police assure me they are doing everything as fast as they can, but in my eyes, it's not fast enough. I feel a little on edge and do my best not to take my anger out on Willow. I don't tell her, but someone is already at the facility Ashton is staying at, talking to her.

All we need her to do is change her statement. My father and Brett assured her they wouldn't press charges, and the police say that as long as Brett is okay with the outcome, the state won't charge her for making a wrong statement either.

After the police are finally gone, Willow and I are left alone in her room again. Part of me wants to hold her all day while the other wants to go to my family's estate and wait for any news regarding my brother. When my phone starts to ping every five seconds with emails, calls, and texts from my mom and dad, I finally decide it's time to go.

As if Willow can read my mind, she stirs on my chest, where she's been sprawled out for a good while. The last thing I want to do is leave right now, but I have to.

"I need to go, Willow. I hate to leave you, but I really need to go."

"I know," she murmurs softly. Through her thick lashes, she peeks up at me, her eyes still swollen and red from all the crying she did this morning.

"Are you going to be okay here?" I don't know why I even ask. That's such a stupid question. After the shit with Nate yesterday, his confession to raping Ashton, and the fact the police have zero leads on where he is, I doubt she's anywhere close to being *okay*.

Of course, despite all of that, she gives me a nod. "I'll be fine."

She rolls to the side, so her body is lying on the bed and not on top of me. I miss her body the moment we lose touch. Leaning over, I kiss her on the forehead and get up to put my shoes on. I can't believe how quickly our relationship has changed. How quickly she went from hating me to needing me. Or maybe she always needed me, but she is just now ready to admit it.

"I'll call you later, okay?"

"Okay, I'm going to try to reach my father and see if he can take me to Ashton."

"Maybe you can ask Alice to drive you instead?" After I saw her father almost hit her yesterday, I'd rather she not be alone with him today, or ever. Willow nods in agreement, obviously, I don't have to give her an explanation.

"I'll call Alice," she confirms, grabbing her phone.

I slip out of the room while Willow makes the call to her friend. I have to force my legs to move, taking each step further away from her. I am torn between wanting to stay with her and wanting to go home. My head says to go home, but the rest of my body wants to stay.

My phone pings again, as if to give me another sign that I need to leave. Checking my messages, I read the words I've so long hoped to read.

Dad: She confessed everything. Brett was released.

On the way to my parents' house, I break every speed limit there is. Pulling into the driveway thirty minutes later, I come to a halt with my tires squealing. I kill the engine and open the door at the same time. There are two cars I don't recognize parked out front, and I wonder who all is here.

I half run toward the front door. When my foot touches the

first step of the porch, the door flies open. I look up, expecting either one of my parents to be there ready to yell at me for not coming earlier. Instead, I find a large body filling out the door frame. All the pressure on my shoulders, the anger, and hate, it fades to the background.

In all his glory, my brother stands before me with a huge smile on his face, one so similar to mine.

"It's about time, little brother," Brett grins, only looking a little different since the last time I saw him. The words have barely left his lips before I'm lunging myself at him. Our chests clash together, his body weight knocking the air out of me.

"Brett, you're home," I tell my brother, who I haven't been able to hug for two years. Every broken piece of my life seems to be mending itself back together. I can breathe without being weighed down by my rage.

"I am, and I'm so fucking happy to see you, brother!" He exclaims, releasing me and moving out of the doorway so that I can come inside. As soon as I'm in the house, I spot my parents sitting in the huge family area. I've never seen either of them smiling so big. Next to them are sitting two men in suits. I remember them from the trial, they were Brett's lawyers.

"Here is my other son," Dad gets up from the couch and walks over to me. He slaps a hand onto my shoulder, squeezing it tightly. I'm still a little pissy over the way he treated Willow last night, but I let it pass. I don't want to ruin Brett's homecoming.

"I heard you're the reason I'm out..." Brett snickers, "Dad has only said ten thousand times how proud of you he is."

Proud of me? "I didn't do anything," I mumble, not really. Nate squealing to Willow is what saved Brett. Which reminds me, I need to find that fucker and rearrange his face.

"Oh, stop, Parker, you know if it wasn't for you and your antics with the youngest Bradford girl, that we wouldn't have gotten your brother out. Your commitment to making that girl understand her place in our world is what saved him." He chuckles, his attention drifting to my brother.

I can't believe my ears. Is he insinuating that I made Nate attack Willow? Before I can think more about it, he continues.

"You should have been at the gala. The dress he put her in. I don't think there was one person in that banquet hall that didn't assume she was a whore. Your brother made a complete sideshow out of her. It was glorious, and the look on her father's face when he saw her was even better."

"You're with Willow?" My brother asks, his eyebrows puckering together in confusion. I open my mouth to speak, but what the hell do I tell him. *Yes? No?* I mean, we aren't official; I really don't know what we are at all. I don't know what the hell is going to happen now, but I don't think I'll be able to let her walk away, not after everything that's happened between us. She's mine.

"Of course, he's not *with* her. He was using her; he wouldn't make a stupid choice like that." My father speaks for me, and his words sting against my skin. I was using Willow, and she was using me, but now, now we're even, or at least I hope we are.

Brett's eyes darken, and I wait for him to give me the whole treat others the way you want to be treated talk, but he doesn't say anything else.

"Ashton confessed to having had consensual sex with Brett that day. She told the police that it was Nate who raped and beat her after Brett left. They're currently looking for him. Are you sure that you don't want to press charges against her? You have a right, son? Two years of your life lost, for something you didn't do. The lawyers are still here, it's not too late."

The air in my lungs stills. *Fuck.* I promised Willow nothing would happen to her sister. If Brett presses charges... Damnit. This is all a fucked-up mess. I want to tell Brett not to do anything but would understand completely if he did.

Seconds feel like hours as my parents and I stare up at Brett, waiting for his response.

"Enough has happened already. Ashton has been hurt plenty, and while I was wrongfully accused, I'm free now, and that's all that matters."

I damn near sag to the floor with relief. It never bothered me before, the thought of hurting Willow. It was a thrill, a funny little game, but now it's like her heart is an extension of my own, her feelings are mine. If something hurts her, it hurts me.

Dad grits his teeth, his eyes bleeding into Brett's. I can see how pissed off he is over his choice. He wants to bring the Bradfords down, and that means Willow too. Would I be able to stand by and watch them do that?

"Whatever you want, son," our father tsks, but something tells me, it will never be whatever we want. It never has been whatever we want, and now that Brett is free, I'll be forced to make a decision. I have to choose between Willow and my father.

The question is. Do I want Willow for more than revenge?

19

WILLOW

The room still smells like Parker, even hours after he's left. Or maybe his scent is just permanently ingrained into my mind now. I don't know. What I do know is that having his smell around me soothes the ache surging throughout my chest.

I can't believe the last twenty-four hours are real.

Everything seems like a dream, a nightmare really. I'm still trying to make sense of it all, to line up the puzzle pieces in my head. Ashton swore it was Brett, she looked me straight in the eyes and swore to me. Had I known it wasn't him…

Guilt eats away at my insides, and that sick feeling I've had all day intensifies.

She's never lied to me. Truth is, when we were little, every time she tried to lie to me, I knew. She's a terrible liar. The worst, so how did I not see it, that time? And why lie in the first place? She could have told me. It wouldn't have changed anything at all. I wasn't the enemy in all of this, and I'm still not.

Holding my head in my hands, I try to calm myself down. It feels like the room is spinning all around me.

Since the moment Parker left, I've been trying to call her at the facility, since Alice didn't pick up, but each time I call, they tell me she can't come to the phone right now. And as much as I hate our father, I even resorted to calling him, but strangely, my calls have been going straight to voicemail.

What the hell is going on?

Not knowing what is happening and being forced to sit and wait is killing me. Almost as much as the thought of what I have done. I helped put an innocent man in prison. Two years of his life are gone, and I am partially to blame for that. I don't know how to deal with it. And even worse, I am in a somewhat relationship with his brother. At least, I think I am. I don't know what Parker and I are, but we are certainly something.

God, could this get any more complicated. All this time, he was right, he was right about his brother, and I really was a liar. I feel compelled to apologize, to beg for forgiveness. I did this. I was an accomplice. Why did Ashton lie? Why did she tell me it was Brett when it was Nate?

Having all these questions, without a single answer in sight, is making it hard for me to function. The hours pass slowly. All night, I sit in my room, every little sound terrifying me. I wonder if Nate is going to come back. If something bad is going to happen to me? Sleep doesn't come, and I don't hear from Parker, or my father, or Ashton, which only makes me worry more.

After a long while, I curl up into a ball and cry until there isn't a single tear left to cry. I cry for my sister mainly, and for Brett, and for Parker and me because had Ashton not lied things, might have been different between us.

I finally fall asleep but come awake not long after, when my phone starts to ring somewhere in the sheets. It could be my father or Ashton. Panicked, I feel around the bed until my fingers find the phone. I don't know why, but seeing my father's name flash across the screen makes me feel like something terrible is going to happen or already has. *No.* Answer the phone, I tell myself. Shoving the feelings away, I hit the green answer key and bring the phone to my ear.

"Dad, is everything okay? I've been calling you all night." The words rush past my lips.

"Willow, I... I don't know how to say this..." The dread in his voice, it clings to me through the speaker. My father hasn't sounded this way since the night of my mother's passing, so why... falling down on me like acid rain, I gasp into the phone.

"What happened? Is Ashton okay? Please, tell me she is okay? Did they press charges?" Every worry known to mankind pops into my head. All I want to know is that she's okay and that I can talk to her. Please, god, let her be okay.

"Willow, Ashton is dead." I can hear the words he's saying, but I don't comprehend them. It's like my brain is refusing to compute.

"What?" I whisper.

"She committed suicide last night. She left a note, but I'm not sure you need to read it right now. I'm in the process of making funeral arrangements. I'll call you when it's time for the funeral." He... I don't understand. What happened? Committed suicide? How? Why? She was in a facility being monitored by nurses and doctors? How did she kill herself?

"I... I don't understand..." A coldness sweeps through my bones, and inside my chest, I can feel my heart cracking. Every beat breaking it a little bit more.

"She's dead, Willow. She is gone, and she's not coming back. I know it's hard in the beginning, but this isn't our first time losing a family member, so I expect us to bounce back from this with ease. We will do the funeral and then carry on with our lives."

The phone slips out of my hand and lands on the floor with a crack. I don't move to pick it up, I don't move at all. I just stand there trying to make sense of the words I just heard. Dead. Suicide. Ashton. Gone. They're all just words, but the meaning behind them is so powerful and soul-crushing they might as well be grenades. Inside my chest, my heart cracks.

The sound is loud and makes it hard for me to breathe.

Ashton is gone... my sister is dead.

My sister is dead and I... I can't bring her back. I can't fix this. Everything I did was for nothing. In the end, I didn't protect her. I fed her right to the monsters. I'll never forgive myself, never.

～

THREE DAYS HAVE PASSED... or maybe four? The days pass in a blur when you don't eat and sleep like a normal person. I'm in some hotel a few towns over from Blackthorn. I couldn't bear seeing or talking to anyone, so I'm hiding out here like the coward I am. I don't know what I'm going to do anymore, but I do know I can't go back there right now.

It took me a few hours to really understand when my father told me about Ashton's death. It took me even longer to grasp what he said after that... *this isn't our first time losing a family member, so I expect us to bounce back from this with ease.*

My father is a psychopath, that's the only explanation for his actions and words. Who is so composed and unaffected by death, by losing their child?

I thought about calling Parker more than once, but I always chickened out. I don't know where we stand after all of this, but I'm too scared to find out right now, too fragile to face him. I checked my phone yesterday right before it went dead. He texted and called a few times, but I ignored them all. Now I'm kind of regretting that I had.

My dad has sent me only one text message, and that was two days ago. He was letting me know when and where the funeral is going to be. Aside from that, he hasn't cared to contact me to see if I'm okay.

Because of this, I hate him a little more than I did before. Scratch that, a lot more, more than I ever thought was possible. I don't see myself ever having a relationship with that man again. If I never see or hear from him again, I'll be a happier person.

The games, the terror, the fear, the fact that someone died... My eyes fill with tears for the millionth time. I can't think about this now. Not ever.

The days have ticked by one right after the other, and I've counted them down with dread. I know Ashton's service is tomorrow, but I don't know if I can bring myself to go. I'd much rather say my goodbyes on my own, and not with a hundred people who didn't care about her, standing in the room.

I feel so guilty, the shit with Brett, and now my sister's death. It all lingers over my head, seconds away from crashing down on me. I feel like I'm in one of those old *Road Runner* cartoons, a large anvil looming over me, ready to squish me like a bug.

My stomach growls, reminding me that I haven't eaten anything in... way too long. I don't even remember. I uncurl myself from the fetal position, which I've been in for the better part of today. Sitting up, I stretch my aching limbs. Realizing how dry my mouth is, I reach for the water on the nightstand, only to realize it's empty. Eventually, I'm going to have to piece myself back together again, but that day isn't going to be today.

I'm reaching for the phone to call room service when a loud knock sounds against the door. My finger grazes the phone. Wait, did I already call and order room service? Or are they just checking on me to make sure I'm not dead yet? Stunted like a deer caught in the headlights of a moving vehicle, I sit there, my eyes on the door.

The knock comes again, this time a little harder than before, and that noise is enough to get me to snap out of it. Slowly crawling out of bed, I walk toward the door. I'm a few feet away when I hear his voice.

"Open the damn door, Willow, or I will kick it in. You might be able to hide from everyone else, but you can't hide from me."

In an instant, I'm grabbing the door handle, my heart lunging in my chest, thumping so hard it almost hurts. *He came for me.* I don't know why, but that brings me a tiny bit of joy. I shouldn't be happy about seeing him. He doesn't deserve me, but more so, I don't deserve him, or anyone else. But I can't help but hold on to that tiny bit of glee, the happiness it brings me, that he is here.

Unlocking the deadbolt, I pull the door open to find Parker standing on the other side of it. One arm propped up on the door frame as if he's been waiting for me to open up for hours instead of seconds. Drinking in his perfect face, I don't know if I want to slap or hug him. The scowl he gives me is one I've seen many times before.

"Why aren't you answering your phone?" Looking me up and down, his blatant anger melts into concern. The struggle in his eyes tells me he wants to take me into his arms, but something is stopping him. Probably the way I look right now. "You look terrible," he mumbles as if he could read my mind.

"I feel like shit too."

"I'm sorry about your sister," he winces, genuine empathy in his tone. "Do you mind if we come in?"

We?

Without waiting for my answer, he drops his arm and walks into the room. I'm flabbergasted by his presence, and even more by the intense tone of his voice. I mentally prepare myself to respond to him when a shadow appears in the doorway. Something tightens in my chest when my eyes land on Brett's dark ones.

"Hello, Willow," he greets, and steps over the threshold.

"Hi," I whisper, my lips trembling.

"I'm sorry about Ashton." He frowns, and I nod. I'm not ready to have this conversation, where everyone apologizes and says sorry for your loss. I'd rather they never have to say anything. I'd rather my sister be alive. Too bad, we don't always get what we want.

Closing the door, I walk back inside and sit on the bed. Parker comes to sit beside me while Brett remains standing, his hands shoved into the front pockets of his jeans. I stare down at my joined hands that rest in my lap. I need to apologize, at least try and make things right.

"I'm sorry," I murmur, looking up at Brett.

"It's okay, you didn't know any better. You were trying to help your sister. I don't blame you at all." The sincerity in his voice hits me hard. Like a bus running me over.

"Truthfully, Brett, I'm sorry. I didn't... If I had known, I wouldn't..." Tears fill my eyes, and the guilt is overwhelming, suffocating me. I did this to him. I took two years of his life away.

Parker's hand comes to rest against mine, the warmth of his touch pulls me from my thoughts, and I direct my attention to him. He's never been so kind and tender before. For a moment, I allow myself to think about what's going to happen in the future. Is there room for Parker and me in this crazy world?

"The funeral is tomorrow. Are you not going to go?" Brett asks.

"I'm not sure. I don't want to stand in a room with a bunch of people weeping over her. People who didn't know or care about her."

He nods and looks down at the floor, his face expressionless. Before everything happened, I thought he and Ashton might get married. Our father was all about that relationship, of course. He was ready to marry his daughter into the Rothschild empire after the first date. Despite my father being pushy, I thought they had something real going on. I don't know, and I guess I never will now, but I really did think that they loved each other.

"How did you find me?"

"I asked your dad. He checked where you used your credit card last, and it was this hotel," his words make me happy and sad at the same time. Parker cared enough to find me here, cared enough to go to my father. But the fact that my dad knows where I am and can't bring himself to come by or even call me... a shudder ripples down my spine.

"I know this must be hard for you, but you need to come back to Blackthorn, you already missed a bunch of classes." Parker's voice holds authority, his face morphing into a little bit of the old Parker, and I can't help but wonder if he would be this way if we were alone right now. What he is not understanding is that he doesn't have that kind of hold on me anymore.

Shaking my head, I tell him, "No, I'm not coming back."

That must strike a nerve because his grip on my hand turns painful, "Don't be stupid, of course, you are."

I don't even wince. All I do is frown because that's the only thing I can seem to get my lips to do. "The only reason I attended that school was so my dad would pay for Ashton to stay in a better rehab facility. He told me I needed to *befriend* people and get invited to functions so he could have access to his old business partners again. That is the one and only reason I agreed to go. Now that, that reason is gone..." I trail off, on the verge of crying again.

"What about me?"

A lump forms in my throat. "I was a means to an end for you. We're even now." The words hurt me as much to say as I know they hurt him to hear.

That perfect jawline of his flexes, "We aren't *even*, not even close."

Shaking my head, I dismiss his statement. I don't have it in me to fight with him. Not right now. I'm not going back though. Not now, or ever.

Silence fills the room, and my stomach starts to grumble loudly.

"When was the last time you ate?"

I shrug, "I don't know, a couple of days."

"Jesus," Parker shakes his head and then pulls his phone out. "I'm going to go downstairs and get something to eat from the restaurant. I'll be right back. I need a minute to think anyway." When he lets go of my hand, a coldness sweeps through me. I hate this rift that's forming between us, but what am I supposed to do? How else should I feel?

He leaves the room, the sound of the door clicking as it closes startles me, and I look up and realize that Brett is still here. Leaning against the small desk, I can feel him watching me. The heat of his gaze penetrates through my skin. The predatory way he's looking at me makes me want to get up and run out of the room, but I grip onto my knees and remain seated.

He's just angry, upset over what happened.

"You are just as beautiful as your sister was, just as stupid too," he grins, and I feel like the world has been turned upside down. I feel off-balance, confused, and scared, really scared. It's not even his words that scare me, it's the look in his eyes that has a shiver running down my spine. His eyes are cold and empty, completely void of all emotions. And no emotions is worse than anything, worse than anger. It means deep down he's unreachable. It means I should run, scream.

He takes a step toward me, and I instinctively scoot back on the bed, trying to get away from him. Parker will be here any second... I tell myself.

"Too bad your sister killed herself before I could have a little fun with her again, you know, for old times sake."

"B-but... Nate..." I stutter, confused, so very confused.

"Yeah, Nate was there too, he was just smarter than me and put on a condom. All I had to do was put on a fucking condom..." He takes another step closer, and again, I move further away. Or at least, I try to. "Her pussy was just too good, and I paid the price..."

With my pulse thundering in my ears, I shuffle closer to the edge of the bed. I prepare myself for my next move, taking my eyes off him for a fraction of a second. In that second, Brett lunges forward, his fingers digging into my ankle. A scream catches in my throat when, with a sharp tug, he pulls my body back toward him.

"This time, I'll make sure I don't leave any evidence, not even a body."

I squeeze my eyes closed as he descends on me, his fingers sinking into my hips so harshly it feels like he's crushing the bone. Pain radiates through me, and inside my head, I pray. Pray, that Parker returns before he gets the chance to end me. Then again...maybe Parker's just as big of a monster as his brother. Perhaps he's in on it.

20

PARKER

I don't know what the fuck I expected to find here. Did I really think she would come back just for me? Did I think she would jump into my arms and be happy to see me?

What about me?

It took a lot to even say those words, and her answer was nothing but a kick in the nut sack. My chest still hurts from that kick. I have to remind myself that this is partially my own fault. I should have taken better care of her. I should have figured out why Willow was in Blackthorn, and I should have known what was going on with Ashton.

I let my need for revenge cloud my mind, and I got sloppy. I should have been smarter than that, but instead, I got caught up in my hunger for vengeance.

We're even now. I almost laugh at the thought. Even. That's what she thought this was... that what I felt for her was only revenge. I guess I would have to show her otherwise, then again, I thought I had shown her. I thought she could feel the change in me.

Sitting in one of the booths at the restaurant, I wait for my order. Seeing her so broken, so damn shattered. It did me in. It made me feel like I hadn't felt in two years. Yes, I set my brother free, but in doing so, killed someone else. I broke Willow.

"Your food is ready," the hostess calls me over to the bar interrupting my thoughts before they spiral out of control. I get up and take the bag she gives me.

"Thanks," I mutter before heading out of the door, through the lobby and into the elevator. The doors pings open on the fifth floor, and I step out. I knock on Willow's door, an uneasy feeling settling in my stomach.

Maybe I shouldn't have come here. Maybe I should give her some more time.

A moment later, Brett opens the door, and the feeling in my gut expands. Something is off. My pulse pounds in my throat, and I grip the bag harder in my closed fist.

"I have a surprise for you," Brett grins, but there is something weird about that grin, something unnatural. His lips are pulled up in a grin, but his eyes are murderous. I know that look, that feeling... it's...

"What—" The word gets lodged in my throat when Brett steps aside, and I peer into the room. My eyes bulge out of my head, and I almost drop the bag of food when I see Willow. I think I'm going to be sick.

She is sprawled out on the bed, gagged and tied up. Her face white as the sheet she is lying on. Big fat tears slip down the side of her face, and all I want to do is run to her and untie her, but something feels very dangerous about this whole situation. Something tells me that treading lightly is my best bet here.

"What the fuck, Brett?" I seethe, barely holding my rage back.

"I know, it's not a good idea to do this here, but I couldn't wait," Brett tells me as if I knew that this was the plan all along.

Walking inside, I close the door, the sound making Willow

jump against the mattress. She looks at me with pleading eyes, struggling with all her strength against the restraints. How the fuck do I defuse this situation? Does she think I did this? Fuck, I'm angry and confused, but above anything else, I have to get him to let her go. No matter what. Even if I have to play along. I'll protect her.

"You need to explain this whole thing to me, Brett, what the hell is going on here? I thought you were innocent. Why are you tying her up?"

"I figured Dad told you the truth by now."

"What truth?" I try to keep my eyes on him, but Willow's whimpering makes it damn near impossible. Each sound, a knife slicing through my skin.

"Nate and I were both there that night. Ashton told me it was over, that she didn't want to see me anymore. Told me I was too controlling. That bitch had to ruin everything. We were perfect for each other, and she had to ruin it all." He shakes his head, disappointment dripping from every word he speaks.

I let the fact that he just admitted to raping Ashton sink in for one single second. If it weren't for me, Willow wouldn't be here right now. She wouldn't be in danger; her sister might still be alive. *He did it.* I thought... I thought he was innocent. This whole time, I blamed someone else. I directed all my anger toward the wrong person.

And my father... he knew too. He knew, and he still treated Willow the way he did? I'll have to deal with him later, but right now, I need to concentrate on Brett.

Looking up at him, it becomes harder not to lash out. He wore his mask so well. Hid his darkness like a second skin. Anger burns through me at the speed of lightning, rushing to the surface, zinging through every cell. Out of the corner of my eye, I can see Willow's petite form shaking. I have to end this... I have to...

"And what are we exactly planning to do here?"

Hating You 181

Brett shrugs, "Just having some fun with her. Don't worry, I brought condoms. Not making that mistake again," he chuckles. He fucking chuckles. He has to be fucking crazy if he thinks I'm going to let him fuck her.

"I don't know if this is a good idea. Like you said, this is a hotel. What if someone hears?" *Defuse the situation.*

"That's why I gagged her. We'll put a pillow over her face for good measure." I can't believe my brother's words. I've looked up to him since I can remember. I'm not a good person by any means, but this, the man he has become, is something else entirely. Where I walk a fine line between right and wrong, he's completely gone, a lost cause. There is no right or wrong with him. There is just what he wants, and that's it.

"Still, we shouldn't do this. Not here."

"Don't tell me you're enamored by her pussy?" He rolls his eyes, "Don't want to share her with me? What happened to brothers share everything?"

It takes everything in me to let my next sentence escapes my mouth, "Fine, I'll share." As I say the words, I force a grin, hoping that it's enough to convince him.

Willow starts to thrash, the bed creaking with every shift of her body. I wish she didn't have to hear that, and I hope like hell that when this is over, she believes that I did this to protect her.

Like an evil villain, he rubs his hands together in excitement. "Great, let's begin."

My brother turns his back to me and heads to the bed, toward Willow... *my* Willow. *Mine.* That one single word resonates through me, ripping through the tissue and bone, branding into my heart. Mine. She is mine. I know what I have to do.

Time seems to slow down. He only takes one step, but a million things are running through my mind. A million scenarios play out in my head all within that one step. *Do it.*

And then, I strike. Like a wild animal, I pounce on Brett's back. My arms circle his neck, and I pull him down into my chest, trying to get a good enough grasp to cut off his air supply. Immediately he struggles against my hold. Struggles so much so, that I almost lose my grip, but all I have to do it glance over at the fragile creature lying on that bed, and a newfound vigor fills my veins. He might be bigger than me, but he doesn't have a reason to fight.

"You fucking asshole," Brett manages to say, his voice strained and breathless. Using his body weight, he makes us sway, and with a kick against the bed, he propels us backward. Before I can think, my back is slamming into the corner of the TV cabinet, knocking the wind straight out of me. Gritting my teeth, I put everything into keeping my hold on him.

"You're the asshole, I fought for you, and you were guilty the whole time," I grit into his ear and tighten my arm around his neck. He makes a choking sound, and I have to drown out the noise, concentrating on Willow instead. Dark hair. Haunting green eyes. My world. My life. I squeeze tighter, feeling Brett's movements slow, the fight in him withering away with each second. My muscles burn, and my jaw clenches so hard I can hear my molars grinding together.

Beads of sweat drip down my face, and a moment later, the room falls silent, and Brett's body goes slack in my hold. As soon as he is out, I let go of him and check his pulse. I want to knock him out, not kill him, well, I kinda want to kill him, but I'm smart enough to know that doing that will leave me without Willow.

When I confirm that he is still alive, I dash to the phone, pick it up and call the front desk.

The moment someone picks up, I yell, "We need the police and an ambulance in room 519. Now!" I slam the receiver back on the station and turn to Willow.

My fingers shake as I start to undo the tape he used to tie

her up. He must have had it in his jacket, which means he planned this whole thing. I don't know why, but that makes me feel even worse. I brought him here and left my Willow alone with him. I pull the piece on her mouth off, and as soon as it hits the floor, a loud sob fills the room.

"I'm sorry, Willow, so sorry," I keep saying as I carefully free her from the rest of the tape. When her hands are free, she slings her arms around me, pulling me closer and burying her face into my chest.

"Oh, god, I thought... I thought..." She heaves in-between sobs.

"Shhh," I try to soothe her, "I know, you don't have to explain it to me."

"I didn't know," she whimpers.

"I didn't know either. You have to believe me, Willow. I had no idea. I thought he was truly innocent." I hiss, my voice plagued with emotion. "I'm so sorry. Everything I did to you. Everything my family did to you. I'm sorry, so fucking sorry." I hold onto her a little tighter, wishing I could just take her and disappear into the darkness.

21

WILLOW

Sitting in Parker's car at the edge of the cemetery, we wait until everybody is gone. I feel cold, every inch of my flesh frozen. Will it be like this forever? Will I feel this way forever? I watch my father from afar, seeing through his mask right away. He is playing the role of the grieving father well, but not well enough to fool me.

Beneath the coldness, pure burning rage consumes me. I hate my father, and I can say that without a single sliver of remorse. He might be my father, but he's nothing close to being the daddy, he leads everyone to believe. This is the end, the freedom I always wanted is mine, but at the expense of one of my loved one's lives. A tightening forms in my chest as I think about how alone I am. I have no one, nothing. It is just me now. It hasn't been that long, and I already miss her. I miss her so much it feels like that empty space inside me will never be filled again.

When every last person has finally left, Parker turns to me. "Are you ready?"

I nod, even though I don't feel ready. Holding onto the flowers in my hand a little tighter, I wait for Parker to move first.

He gets out of the car, comes around, and opens my door. He has to help me out because my body matches the state of my mind right now; confused, broken, and weak. Looping my arm into his, I let him lead me to my sister's grave. She was laid to rest beside my mother. Another reminder of how much I've already lost, though I am happy that they are together again, even if it's just here.

Staring down at the freshly moved dirt, I wonder what I should say. Words won't change what happened, they won't bring her back.

"I'm sorry," I bite my lip hard enough to make it bleed while attempting to hold back the sob from ripping from my throat. "I'm sorry for letting you down. I'm sorry for not fighting hard enough for you. You were all I had, and I let you down."

Parker's hand rubs slow, gentle circles against my back, reminding me that he is still here, that he wants me. But that's not enough. That's not going to bring her back to me.

"I miss you so much. It hasn't been that long, but it feels like it's been, and I know it's only going to get worse." The wind blows, and my body sways with the movement. "I'll get you justice and make everyone who did you wrong pay."

And I will. I'll make sure Nate and Brett get what's coming to them. Justice will be served. On shaky legs, I walk forward and place the flowers on her grave. I hold back the tears and take a step back.

"You may be gone big sister, but you will not be forgotten," I whisper. Parker's strong arm wraps around my middle, and he pulls me back into his chest. The warmth of his body seeps into mine, and I start to shiver.

What happens next? I'm so lost now. I have nothing, nowhere to go, nothing to look forward to.

"It's getting cold," Parker whispers softly into the shell of my ear.

"What...what do I do now?" The tears start to fall, staining my cheeks.

"Let's talk about it," he says, and I start to sob as I walk back toward the car, each cry a silent scream for help. I'm drowning in misery and sadness, and the water keeps rising. How will I survive? Parker opens the car door and helps me in. I wipe at my tired eyes, wanting the tears and pain to stop. Entering the car, he turns it on and blasts the heat. Then as if I weigh nothing more than a small child, he tugs me across the center console and into his lap.

I don't fight him, needing his warmth, his support. Placing my head against his chest, I focus on the familiar beat of his heart.

Thump. Thump. Thump.

Running his fingers through my hair, Parker speaks low, "I know it's going to be hard for you, but I want you to come back to Blackthorn with me. I want you, really want you. Not in a revenge kind of way, or even obsession...though I am obsessed with you." The last part comes out in a whisper. His confession should make me smile, and it would if I could manage to smile right now.

"I can't. I can't afford the tuition there, and the only way my father will pay for it is if I act as his pawn, and I refuse to have anything to do with him. I don't want to be caged anymore. I want to be free."

"I..." the tremble in his voice causes me to pull back, and I stare up at him through teary eyes. He looks conflicted, pained. "I... I love you, Willow, and I'm trying so hard to give you a choice, even though I want to tell you that you're going to stay with me. The thought of losing you. It kills me. It makes me manic. In my mind, you're mine, always have been, since the moment I laid eyes on you."

He... he loves me? My gaze widens, and I feel his words. I feel them moving through me. But is his love enough?

"I can't go back, Parker," I confess.

"You can. I'll pay for your tuition. You can live with me in my house. I'll take care of you. If you let me. If you want me."

If I want him? Doesn't he understand that the only reason I haven't fallen completely off the wagon is because he's holding me in place, keeping me grounded?

"I'm going to give you a choice. If you don't want this, then I'll help you go somewhere else. If you don't want me, I'll pay for you to go to another school, find you somewhere to live. You won't have to worry about money or your father. You won't have to worry about me either."

He isn't saying what I think he is, is he? He's not giving me up?

"You would really do that for me?" It almost sounds too good to be true. Like a trick, but what would he get from it?

"Yes, I would do anything for you. If you chose to come home with me, things will be different, I promise. No more games, no more using each other. It's just going to be us, you and me, trying to make it work. So, what do you say?"

His offer is so tempting, and everything I've ever wanted to hear him say. But I'm still scared, still afraid.

Grabbing my face, he pulls me to him, forcing me to look in his eyes.

"I love you, Willow, and if you come with me, I will treat you like my queen. I will never let anyone hurt you. You have always been mine, but now, I will be yours too. You will be my equal. Please..." He pleads, and that's enough to shatter the fear surrounding my heart.

"I want you, Parker, and I love you. I'll come with you."

With a huge smile on his lips, he kisses me, squeezing me to his chest, making me feel that nothing can touch us. Not his parents. Not our past. Together we're invincible.

Hate turned to love, and my bully became my salvation.

EPILOGUE

Parker

Sitting in the cafeteria with Willow and Warren, I think back on the last six months. How much my life has changed, how much I, as a person, have changed. The anger I had before is gone now, replaced with a violent love for Willow. She completes me in every way, and I'm thankful every fucking day that I wake up and see her beside me in bed. It's why I can't regret the path that led us here, even though I hate what my brother made me become, I hate that I fought so hard for him and did some questionable things all to make Willow pay. How she forgave me, I don't know. After all, she wasn't the liar, I was, by default.

I press a kiss into her hair and inhale her scent, *mine*, all mine.

"I have to get going. I have an early class." Willow starts to pull away, and all I want to do is tell her no and pull her into my chest and take us home so I can ravage every inch of her.

"I can walk you," I tell her as she stands, grabbing her tray.

"No, stay and finish your lunch. I'll meet you at home later. Bring dinner, please." Her eyes lighten, and I can see the happiness in them. Before Nate was caught, I wouldn't let her out of my sight, but two months ago, they finally got him. He is currently rotting in jail where he belongs.

My Brett's freedom was short-lived, he was thrown back in jail the same day he tried to attack Willow. I haven't talked to him since, and I'm not planning to do so anytime soon, maybe not ever again.

Willow's father tried for weeks to contact her, to weasel his way back into her life, especially after he found out we were dating and moved in together. After I gave Willow the letter that Ashton left for her—I'd made her father hand it over the day of the funeral—that he tried to conceal, she cut all ties, thank God! It took her a while to get over the contents of the letter, knowing what had happened and how much she'd kept to herself was tough on Willow, but it did give her some much-needed closure, and she now has a reminder of her sister's love for her. The one good thing is that it could be used as evidence against both Brett and Nate, those sick fucks should be locked up for quite some time. I made sure her father got the message to leave her alone.

I haven't talked to my own father either, and I'm not planning on doing so ever again. He is partly to blame for all of this and I hope that one day he gets what he deserves too. My mother however comes around once a week. She swears up and down that she didn't know, and I believe her, so I don't mind having her be a part of my life.

I'm still working on grasping the extent of Brett's actions. It's hard to understand what Brett had done, and it's even harder to admit the things I have done. I've apologized to Willow a thousand time for treading her the way I did, and yet, it doesn't seem enough. I don't know if it will ever be enough.

Leaning down, Willow kisses me, her lips lingering on mine, and the alpha in me bursts to the surface. I grip onto her hips and pull her into my body.

"I'm going to devour you later, every inch," I whisper against her lips, my cock growing hard when I see the twinkle of excitement in her emerald gaze.

"I look forward to it," she replies and then starts to pull away. I let her go, even though I don't want to. Watching as she walks away, I know I'm the luckiest son of a bitch at this school. After everything we went through, everything I did, how I hurt her, she still wants me. I make it up to her every day, showing her body pleasure, cherishing her, and loving her in a way she deserves to be loved. Like a queen. My queen.

"Tell me again, how an asshole like you managed to snag a girl like her?" Warren's piss and vinegar attitude is starting to get on my last nerve. Lately, he's become less and less of the carefree, funny guy I've known him to be. It's like he has been replaced with a huge grumpy ass.

"Dude, I don't know what the fuck your problem is." I clench my hand into a closed fist and press it against my knee. I really want to slug him, but I promised Willow I would try to be more civilized.

In an instant, Warren's demeanor goes from asshole to pure devil. His gaze darkens, turning to ice, and his jaw clenches so tightly, the edges become sharp enough to cut. I watch as his death stare tracks something off in the distance. He reminds me of a hunter, waiting for its prey to pop back out of the brush.

"What the fuck?" I ask under my breath, following his line of sight. My gaze catches on a petite girl about our age. Even from this distance, I can see that she's pretty, like an angel, with delicate features. She stands talking to one of the professors. She must be new because I've never seen her before. It doesn't make much sense, though, because, with the way Warren is looking at her, I get the impression he knows her.

"Who is she?" I ask him.

Instantly, he snaps out of whatever darkness was holding onto him. "She's no one." His reply is short, snappy, and completely unlike him.

"Dude, she's obviously someone. I've never seen your face change so quickly. It was almost like you were seeing a ghost."

A smile that even makes me cringe pulls at his lips. "That's because I was. She's no one, nothing. Forget you saw her."

Confused, I shake my head, but Warren doesn't give me a chance to respond. In a flash, he's gone from the table, his tray the only evidence that he was here.

What the fuck was that?

Picking the tray up, I lift my gaze to the spot the girl was standing in just a moment ago, only to find that Warren is standing right in front of her. Nearly blocking out my entire view of her, he towers over her like a shadow. She looks uncomfortable, maybe even a little scared as he grabs her by the arm and tugs her through one of the doors that leads out to the garden.

I dump the tray and push Warren and his whiplash behavior out of my mind. Whatever is going on with him, he's going to have to deal with it on his own.

I'm not going to get involved. I finally have my dream girl, and I'm not compromising what we have for anything.

~

Setting down the Chinese takeout on the kitchen counter, I move through the house, trying to find Willow. She's in here somewhere...

"Where are you, baby?"

"Waiting for you," she answers, her soft voice coming from the bedroom. I push the door open and find her lying on the bed...naked. Swallowing my tongue, I drink her in. "I was promised every inch of me would be devoured."

Challenge accepted.

"Fuck, yeah," I grin, already pulling my shirt off and unbuckling my pants. She giggles as I pounce on her, my mouth finding her hardened nipples. I close my lips around one and suck on it hard. Enjoying how it hardens even further as I run my tongue over it. Her fingers disappear into my hair, her nails raking across my scalp as she holds me to her chest. I can feel her touch in my cock.

"I want you on your back," Willow tells me breathlessly, her pretty eyes gleaming.

"Is that so?" I ask a little surprised. She is not usually the one to take charge in the bedroom. Nevertheless, I happily oblige. Rolling over, I lie on my back and watch her as she climbs on top of me, straddling me. Her hands land flat on my stomach, holding herself steady.

"I want to ride you," she confesses.

"You're not going to hear any complaints out of me." Tucking my hands behind my head, I give her all the control. Eagerly she lifts herself and fists my cock in her hand. Her touch makes my eyes roll to the back of my head.

"All afternoon, I thought about this," she whispers as the fat head of my cock brushes against her drenched entrance. She's going to kill me if she doesn't put it in soon.

"Yeah, what did you think about?" I hiss through my teeth, staring up at my queen through hooded eyes.

She bites at her bottom lip, "How it would feel... you entering me, the stretch and little sting, the pleasure..." A shudder ripples through her body as well as my own as she sinks down, her pussy swallowing all eight inches of my cock. It's a damn sight to see, one, only I will ever have the pleasure of seeing. Tossing her head back, she starts to move up and down, up and down. I grit my teeth and become enchanted under her spell as her hips swivel, and her pussy squeezes my cock.

Her tiny nails sink into my abs, and the pain and pleasure mixing together are like the perfect euphoric cocktail.

"Oh, god..." She pants, bearing down on my length. I can feel every flex, every flutter of her fucking perfect womb.

"What is it, baby? What do you need?" I question my voice clouded with carnal need.

"More, I need more." Her big green eyes pierce mine, and I know what she's asking. I know what she needs, but if she wants it, then she's going to have to say it.

"Tell me, tell me what you need," I order, my voice lower than normal. I ache to flip her over, put her on her knees, and take from her until she's screaming for me to stop, but she has to tell me... beg me.

Like an alluring siren, she flutters her eyes at me, "I want you to fuck me. Please, fuck me." A switch flips inside my head, and before I realize it, I'm pulling out of her and moving us around. Grabbing her by the arm, I push her into the mattress face first and secure her arms behind her. She lets out a tiny squeal of excitement that only feeds the hungry beast.

"Because you asked so nicely," I grin, and rut into her with everything I have. She mewls against the sheets as I hold her in place, fucking her without mercy, without care. Showing her that I can be both tender and untamed. Showing her that I can be whatever she needs me to be.

"Parker," she cries out, and I squeeze her arms tighter, pushing her into the mattress with more force. Feeling the pleasure build at the bottom of my spine, I pick up speed, thrusting into her with a ferocity that's wild and primal.

"Be a good girl and come on my fucking cock. Squeeze me nice and tight, and I'll fill you up with my come."

Trying to push back against me, she sighs, and then I feel it, the distinct fluttering of her muscles. She grips me so hard, stars appear before my eyes. I don't stop though. I continue to plow into her, my hips thrusting, my cock hitting the back of her cervix.

Mine. All fucking mine.

"You're mine, all fucking mine. Today, tomorrow, forever..."

With one final thrust, I erupted inside her, going off like a cannon. My toes curl, and I vibrate against her sweat-soaked body. There is nothing like falling apart with her, nothing like feeling my come pulse inside of her.

Releasing her arms, I press open mouth kisses to the flesh. "Are you okay? Was I too rough?" I ask, pulling out of her and flipping her over, so we're facing each other. Her cheeks are pink, and her eyes are sleepy, but there is a smile on her face, and that's all that matters to me. Seeing her smile, seeing her happy.

"No, you were perfect. In fact, next time, I think you should go a little harder," she teases, and my cock jumps to life at the thought.

"Don't tempt me, you still have a hole I haven't claimed yet."

Her gaze softens, and I know she's not ready for me to claim that part of her yet, but someday she will be, and when that time comes, I'll own every single part of her completely, because while Willow was my retribution, she'll always be my forever.

The End

ALSO BY THE AUTHORS

CONTEMPORAY ROMANCE

The Bet
The Dare
The Secret
The Vow

Bayshore Rivals
(Reverse Harem Bully Romance)

When Rivals Fall
When Rivals Lose
When Rivals Love

***

DARK ROMANCE

The Rossi Crime Family
(Dark Mafia Romance)

Convict Me
Protect Me
Keep Me
Guard Me
Tame Me
Remember Me

Also by the Authors

Hating You
Breaking You
(Dark Bully Romance)

***

EROTIC STANDALONES

Runaway Bride
FREE NOVELLA

There Captive
(A Dark Reverse Harem)

Beck and Hallman

BLEEDING HEART ROMANCE

- **f** CASSANDRAHALLMAN
  AUTHORJLBECK

- **Instagram** CASSANDRA_HALLMAN
  AUTHORJLBECK

- **BB** CASSANDRAHALLMAN
  JLBECK

Printed in Great Britain
by Amazon